MARY
WOLF

Books by Cynthia D. Grant

Kumquat May, I'll Always Love You

Phoenix Rising

Keep Laughing

Shadow Man

Uncle Vampire

Mary Wolf

MARY
WOLF

Cynthia D.
Grant

ALADDIN PAPERBACKS

25 Years of Magical Reading

ALADDIN PAPERBACKS
EST. 1972

First Aladdin Paperbacks edition 1997
Copyright © 1995 by Cynthia D. Grant
Aladdin Paperbacks
An imprint of Simon & Schuster
Children's Publishing Division
1230 Avenue of the Americas
New York, NY 10020
Also available in an Atheneum Books for Young Readers edition.
The text of this book was set in Apollo
Printed and bound in the United States of America
10 9 8 7 6 5 4 3 2 1

The Library of Congress has cataloged
the hardcover edition as follows:

Grant, Cynthia D.
Mary Wolf / by Cynthia D. Grant
p. cm.
Summary: Sixteen-year-old Mary tries to keep her family together
as they aimlessly travel the country after her father's business fails
and he starts to change.
ISBN 0-689-80007-X
[1. Family problems—Fiction.] I. Title.
PZ7.G76672Mar 1995
95-2128
[Fic]—dc20

ISBN 0-689-81251-5 (Aladdin pbk.)

*The lines on page vii are from CHILDREN OF DARKNESS by Richard
Fariña © 1966 (renewed) WARNER BROS. INC. All Rights Reserved.
Used by Permission.*

For Erik, my haven and home,
and for Forest

With special thanks to the author's friend
and attorney, Jim DeMartini, who generously
donates his time and expertise with no
thought of compensation.

That's D-E-M-A-R-T-I-N-I.
He's in the phone book.

Now is the time for your loving, dear,
And the time for your company,
Now, when the light of reason fails
And fires burn on the sea.
Now, in this age of confusion
I have need for your company.

from the song "Children of Darkness"
by Richard Fariña

One

It's easy for my mother to shoplift now that she's pregnant. She sails into a store like a pirate ship, her full skirt billowing around her ankles.

I'm at a counter with the little girls tumbling around me, saying to the teenage clerk at the cash register: "Excuse me, do you have any flannel pajamas?"

Flannel? The teenager wrinkles up her forehead as if I'm speaking a foreign language. The kids are a great distraction. They're not in on the act; they're giggling and shrieking. Then somebody's screaming: "She hit me, Mary!"

"She hit me first!"

Meanwhile, Mama's cruising the aisles like a shark, popping stuff inside her exhausted waistband as the teenager twirls a stiff blond curl, saying something like, "Flannel? What do you mean by flannel?"

Then my mother's by the door, calling, "Girls, I'm ready."

"Thanks anyway," I say, and we go outside. My father's in the RV, in the parking lot, reading the business section of that city's newspaper. He follows the tides of the stock market as if he were still a player.

"All set?" he asks as we pile in the door. I herd the kids to the back and buckle their seat belts. My father starts the engine of the Wolfs' Den, and we head into the morning traffic.

My mother is shedding merchandise concealed in the voluminous folds of her clothing: underpants for the girls, men's socks, a lamp, a lamp for God's sake, perfume, earrings. We drive across town to another store. Expertly, invisibly, she harvests the shelves.

We sell the stuff at flea markets, to earn our living.

I say: "How do you expect the kids to know right from wrong when they know you're stealing?"

My father frowns into the rearview mirror. Mama turns around, looking sad.

"I wouldn't call it that, Mary."

"What would you call it?"

She says, "This is a special situation."

"I'll be damned if I'll let my family go hungry." Daddy bites into a stolen doughnut, his breakfast.

"But they see what you're doing—"

"They don't see what I'm doing. They're children, Mary. They're not paying attention."

Although Mama will give birth to her fifth baby soon, she doesn't grasp the nature of children. She thinks they're oblivious blank-eyed dolls. The girls see everything; they're always listening, even the littlest one, Paula, who's three. They're listening right now, even though they look busy eating doughnuts and licking their fingers.

"They're smart," I say. "They know what's going on. But don't listen to me. I'm just a kid."

"Someone sure got up on the wrong side of the bed this morning," Daddy tells Mama. She pats his leg.

We're moving through another big city. After a while they all look the same: gas stations, shopping malls, cars, people. We should've left the campground for the flea market early but Daddy's stomach was bothering him again last night, so he turned off the alarm and we overslept.

The flea market is located on the parking lot of a fairgrounds. Mama goes to the door of a tiny office by the gate and pays a fat woman ten dollars for our space.

Daddy navigates the RV down a row of cars with tables in front of them, covered with junk, old and new. He parks the Wolfs' Den and we set up our tables. I unroll the striped awning over our heads. We'll need it; the sun is blazing.

Quickly, practiced, Mama lays out her wares. People are already crowding around. "We've got lots of bargains today," she tells them.

Clothing and books and housewares here, toys and cassettes and videotapes there. The watches and jewelry are in a locked glass case. Mama wears the key on a chain around her throat.

"How much for that watch?" A man taps the glass.

"Ten," Mama tells him.

"I'll give you six."

"Ten," she insists. He shrugs and walks away. Mama winks at me and says, "He'll be back."

She knows her customers; she reads their faces, divining the depths of their pockets and souls. Soon she is pulling in dollars, making change. I watch the kids while Daddy shops for a new electric razor.

When the kids get bored, I take them inside and make peanut butter and jelly sandwiches. The motor home is like a house on wheels; it has a tiny kitchen with a fridge and stove, beds, chairs, tables, lamps, even a bathroom with a shower. When we can't plug into a hookup, the appliances run off the generator and battery.

I put on the TV. The reception is lousy but the girls don't mind. They watch cartoons.

Outside, Mama argues with a teenage boy who palmed a knife and tried to slip away. Nothing makes Mama angrier than people stealing her stolen goods.

"Put it back or pay for it."

"I didn't take nothing." The boy's sullen face swells. People are staring.

"Put it back!" she says.

He calls her a bitch, throws the knife on the table, and stalks away.

"Kids today," Mama tells one of her customers.

The woman nods. "Ain't it the truth."

I tidy the merchandise that's been tossed around. It makes me cringe to see the antique amber necklace that Mama took from the old lady's house.

She told the woman we were looking for the Walkers. Did she know the Walkers? Old friends of our family. They lived around here someplace.

"I'm sorry, I don't," the woman said. "Used to be I knew all my neighbors. But nowadays, people move around so much."

"I know what you mean," Mama said. "It's a shame."

I stood behind her on the steps, holding Polly in my arms, so she could see we were just a normal family, not maniacs come to rob and kill her.

Not kill her, anyway.

"Oh, I'm so thirsty," Mama said. "Since I got pregnant, it seems like I'm always thirsty. Could I trouble you for a glass of water?"

"No trouble at all. Come in and sit down. You girls can come in, too."

"That's okay, we'll wait outside." It's bad enough doing what I do; I can't stand to watch Mama steal.

We move through the neighborhoods. Do you know the Walkers? We're looking for the Walkers. Old friends of our family. Kids trust Mama; she looks like their mothers. But she fools adults too because oh my goodness, suddenly she feels so faint.

"Come in and sit down. When's that baby due? I'll bring you some water." They leave the room. Then Mama scoops up whatever's in range and pops it into her diaper bag purse: a ceramic ashtray, a crystal vase. Little things that won't be missed until later.

Little things, Mama says. That's all it is. Mary, do you want your sisters to starve?

It makes me sick to see that stuff on our tables. The stamp collection. The music box engraved *June 16, 1967*. A gift for high school graduation? An anniversary present? And the necklace of antique amber beads.

Mama catches me looking at it. "You can have that, Mary. It would be real pretty with your hair."

"I don't want it."

It's lunchtime; Daddy brings hot dogs and sodas. It's hot in the RV. The fan won't work. Mama eats while she sells. "We're doing good," she says. The money belt she wears looks heavy.

My father lies down to take a nap, clutching his stomach. "Too much coffee," he groans. He should see a doctor, but we don't have insurance and they want money up front.

Paula sleeps, too, her hair damp with sweat. Erica and Danielle play the Sorry game Daddy picked up at one of the booths.

I tell Mama I'll take over so she can rest, but she says I sell too cheap. She gets top dollar.

A man and a woman look over our stuff. They match, like the chipmunk salt and peppers she's fingering.

"Look here, hon," she says to him. "These are real cute."

"Uh-huh," he says, examining the tape deck. "This thing work?"

"It works fine," Mama says. "I'll plug it in so you can hear it."

"I'll give you fifteen for it."

"Twenty," Mama says.

"Seventeen."

"Twenty. Firm."

I'm watching the woman. She's staring at the music box. Her face looks funny.

"Joe," she says. "Look." She points it out.

Then she's staring at the digital clock.

"Joseph!" she hisses, and motions him away. They stand at a distance and stare at us and whisper. Their faces change from puzzled to angry.

Mama's selling a package of new socks, telling her customer, "These came in today." But she misses nothing. She sees the couple march off, headed toward the flea market office.

"Mary!" Mama says. We move quickly. Mama sweeps the tables clean, dumping stuff into boxes that we stow in the RV's outside compartments. I roll up and secure the awning.

"Andrew!" Mama calls into the motor home. "We're leaving. Andrew! What's the matter, honey?" She hurries to their bunk. He's lying on his side, clutching his stomach and moaning.

"You're white as a sheet! Your skin feels clammy."

He lurches into the john and throws up. The girls are frozen on their bunks, watching.

"Mary!" Mama's scared. "We've got to go!" She doesn't know how to drive the RV, or even the Jeep chained behind it. Daddy wanted her to learn. "I can't! I just can't!" she'd cried. She's crying now.

I climb behind the steering wheel. "Put on your seat belts," I tell the girls. "Fast."

"I'm thirsty," Polly says.

"Do it now!"

"You're mean, Mary!"

Through the windshield I can see the angry couple talking to the fat woman outside the office, their faces turned in our direction.

"Sit down, Mama." I start the engine. Daddy comes out of the bathroom and lies down, flinging his arms across his face.

I drive slowly through the crowd of people and tables, circling the parking lot, away from the office, looking for an exit. An escape.

"Jesus, there's got to be another way out."

"Mary, don't take the Lord's name in vain," Mama murmurs beside me, her seat belt snug across her massive belly.

I spot another exit. There's a pickup in the way; people are loading a couch into the back.

"We've got to get out of here!" Mama cries. "Go around them!"

The Wolfs' Den is huge and hard to maneuver. I scrape past the pickup truck. The people glare.

"Go!" Mama says. "Go, Mary!"

Where?

It really doesn't matter, when you have no destination.

I pull into the traffic, my armpits prickling, my hands shaking on the steering wheel.

"Isn't it a good thing Daddy taught you how to drive," Mama says.

"It's wonderful," I say. "It's great."

"Andrew," she calls, "how you doing, hon?"

In the rearview mirror I see him wave, signaling that he's okay, keep going.

Keep going is the order of the day. Every day.

The traffic is heavy. I move over to the right, looking for a freeway entrance.

Mama dumps the money belt into her lap. "We did pretty good," she says, counting. "I can't believe how cheap people are. They always want something for nothing."

I get onto the freeway. We leave the city behind. Mama slips off her shoes.

"Ooh, that's better. My feet are so swollen." She rubs her belly. "Put your hand here, Mary. You can feel the baby moving."

"I'm busy now, Mama." I drive and drive. My father sleeps. The kids are quiet. I clench my teeth, holding back the angry words. There's no telling what I'd say to my mother.

"Mary," she says timidly, "I'm sorry, honey. In a city that size, who would've thought that would happen?"

"Yeah, what a coincidence. A million people and you manage to steal from your customers."

"It won't happen again. It's never happened before."

"That's not true. Remember Memphis?"

Probably not. She forgets. The cops asked a bunch of questions and Mama made up this story about kids, teenagers, selling her the stuff and she had no idea it was stolen. It wasn't her fault.

It was all a mix-up. Do we look like the kind of people who would steal? We're just a normal family on vacation.

A vacation that never ends.

"We can't keep this up," I say. "It's just a matter of time before we get nailed."

"Nailed. Who taught you to talk like that? You certainly didn't learn that from Daddy or me."

"Mama, can you get serious for one minute? We're coming to the end of the line here. I can feel it."

"Are we in trouble?" Danielle sounds worried. She's ten years old and knows about jail.

"No, we're not," Mama says. "Everything's fine."

"But Mary said— "

"Don't worry, Danielle. Mama and I were just talking. Why don't you and the girls take a snooze? We'll be on the road for a while."

We're in the country, driving through rolling green hills. We'll need a place to stay for the night. Where should we head? Where are we now?

"I need the map, Mama."

She hands me Arkansas.

"No," I say. "California."

Mama turns on the radio and sings along. Then she says, "I almost forgot." She pulls something from her pocket and says, "Close your eyes, Mary."

11

"Mama, I'm driving."

"Then hold out your hand. Come on, sweetie, hold it out."

The girls aren't sleeping; they crowd close to see. Mama places something cool and smooth on my palm. It's the necklace of antique amber beads.

"Oooh!" the girls say. "Look, Mary! It's pretty."

"I knew you liked it," Mama says, "and today is a very special day."

"It is?"

"It's the twenty-fifth of April! Your birthday!"

"Are you sure?"

"Of course I'm sure! Happy birthday, darling. I'm going to make a cake when we stop for the night."

"With candles?" Erica asks. "And ice cream, too?"

She and Polly sing the birthday song.

I'm surprised it's my birthday. The days roll by, one road leading to another. Flowers bloom beside the freeway. It's springtime again.

I'm sixteen years old today.

Two

Things are looking up. My father has a job. Soon we'll be able to rent a house and go to school again.

We've been staying in a trailer park outside Stockton. The sign on the gate welcomes overnighters, but most of these trailers are here to stay. They have dented tin skirts and flat tires. The cars that towed them have gone to the junkyard. The park is crowded. We were lucky to get a space.

Daddy's working at a big discount store downtown. He's the assistant manager of the camera department. Last night he was in a terrific mood. We laughed around the dinner table.

"There'll be medical benefits, too," he promised, "as soon as I pass my three months' probation."

"That's wonderful," Mama said. "The girls

could use checkups, and I want to get a doctor for the baby. And you've got to have somebody look at your stomach."

"Here it is!" Daddy lifted his shirt. The girls giggled. He says the pain's just an ulcer, from stress.

"You should see this place; it's huge," he said. "They've been looking for a man with my experience. Today Thrifty, tomorrow the world. I'm telling you, Wendy, I've got the magic again." He and my mother smiled at each other and clinked their water glasses together.

Back home in Nebraska, Daddy sold insurance. He had his own office and twelve guys under him. Under him, that's what he always said. We had a two-story house with a big sloping lawn. I remember playing in a fan of silver water, the sprinkler shimmering back and forth.

We had so much money, Daddy bought the RV brand-new; parked it in the driveway and surprised us. Mama's hand went to her throat.

"Andrew, it's enormous! Are you sure we can afford it?"

He laughed and hugged her. "That's my department."

Our last name is Wolf, so he made a sign that says THE WOLFS' DEN and hung it in back, above the license plate. He bought the red Jeep to tow behind it. The motor home handles like a dinosaur and uses a lot of gas. We went camping every summer and took long trips. The back of the RV sprouted colorful stickers from all the amusement parks we visited.

Then things began to change, very slowly at first, like great puffy clouds moving in from the north. The economy was bad. Business fell off. People had no money for insurance. Daddy had to fire six of his salesmen. One day the head office called. Daddy's branch was closed and he was out of a job for the first time since he was eighteen years old.

"Don't worry," he told Mama. "We have money in the savings, and I'll be working again before you know it."

Every night the TV news showed long lines of people standing outside unemployment offices. Daddy mailed off résumés, filled out hundreds of applications, went on job interviews. Came home raging.

"I'm too old!" he roared. "Overqualified! I've got too much experience, that's what they said. They want kids fresh out of college, so they don't have to pay them. I'm telling you, Wendy, the world's gone crazy."

It wasn't his fault. The recession was the problem, all the newspapers said so. We bundled them and sold them to recyclers, along with the aluminum cans we collected.

Mama's parents couldn't help; they'd lost their store and were living on Social Security.

They live in Indiana. We hadn't visited often. They get on Mama's nerves. Daddy's family lived in town. Grandma and Grampa loaned us money. But after a while Daddy didn't want to see them. He was too ashamed. He fought with his sister. Aunt Belle said the recession was the Republicans' fault. No, Daddy said, it was the damn liberals. They were ruining the country. Everybody had their hands out. People would rather go on welfare than work.

"Bullshit," Aunt Belle said at the dinner table. He told her to leave our house and not come back. It wouldn't have happened if he hadn't been drinking. He never drank before he lost his job.

The next day Daddy made an announcement: We were leaving on vacation in the RV, to see this great country of ours.

"It's the perfect opportunity," he explained. "Once I'm working, we won't be able to get away."

"But Andrew, how can we afford it?" Mama asked.

"You leave that to me. Quit worrying, honey."

"We can't just take the girls out of school."

"Why not? Think of the places they'll see! Washington, Gettysburg, the Grand Canyon! All of the places where history's been made. This will be a real education."

It sounded so exciting, no one thought to ask when we'd be home again.

"You girls finish your breakfast. Then we'll have our lessons," Mama says, struggling to make the beds. Her belly gets in the way. Mama and Daddy have the bed up front, with a folding screen for privacy. Our bunks are stacked in back, around the living room space. "Mary, you need to do the laundry. Don't forget to take the towels."

"I thought we were registering for school today."

"Not until we know where we'll be living. Daddy wants to rent a house in the best school district."

Since we left Nebraska, I've been in school off and on. Last year I went for several months, when Daddy had a job in Colorado. The kids at the high school had known each other forever. They treated me as if I were from outer space.

But the teachers were nice and they really helped me. Luckily I'm smart and I catch on quickly. That's not enough; I need a good education. I want to be somebody in this world. I always loved school; the neat rows of desks, the books filled with important information. There were schedules and rules and regulations. I miss that.

"We should start right away. The girls are so far behind."

"No they're not, Mary. They're doing fine. If you really want to help, get that laundry done."

I think Mama will be lonely when we're back in school. And she needs my help to get things done, especially now that a baby's coming.

"Mama, do we have to study?"

Erica would rather watch cartoons. Mama likes to do that, too. But Daddy says education is important; he's bought workbooks and pencils and an old encyclopedia set. At night he makes us watch public-television shows about dolphins and opera and the universe.

"No, we're going to study first," Mama insists. Polly turns on the TV and Mama pretends not to notice. The girls' eyes drift toward the set. While I stuff dirty clothes into pillowcases, Mama has Erica read aloud from a library book we checked out in Arizona. Daddy says you can borrow library books anywhere in the country and put them in a mailbox when you're done. They're mailed back free, like motel keys, he says.

I wonder if that's true.

I cross the park to the Laundromat, past trailers, RVs, campers, even tents. Kids and dogs chase each other through the fog. At the office the manager's telling a man with a bad cough, "You play, you pay. I'm not running a resort."

The Laundromat's deserted. That's when I like it best. In the afternoons it's full of tired women snapping at their kids: Sit still or I'll smack you.

I load the laundry into washers and feed in the quarters. Water gushes in. I add the soap. I forgot to bring a book. I'd run back and get one, but I did that once and the clothes disappeared.

There's not much to read here, mostly old *Watchtower*s. I sit in one of the plastic chairs and look through a real-estate magazine listing local homes for sale.

Watch out, I'm flying, I'm leaving my body, casting off reality like outgrown jeans that bare my ankles and pinch my belly. Look at these houses! Acres of living rooms, miles of skylights. Here's the perfect house for us: five bedrooms, three bathrooms. Three! The girls can have their own rooms and I'll take the guest house, out beside my "very own Olympic-sized pool"! The baby's due soon. She'll need a room. Maybe she could share with Polly. It might be a boy. Daddy says it doesn't matter, but I think deep down he wants a son. Most men do.

When Mama got pregnant, I hoped and prayed we could go back to Nebraska to have the baby. We could stay with Aunt Belle until Daddy found a job. She'd let us, but he'd never ask her. He writes long letters to Grandma and Grampa but he pretends Aunt Belle doesn't exist.

I send her secret postcards and call her collect, or drop in a few coins and talk to her answering machine. "Hi, it's me," I say. "Not much is new. I just wanted you to know we're still alive."

I've even called her at work. She's a nursing supervisor. I hate to bug her at the hospital.

"Don't be silly, Mary! I'm so glad you called! How are you, honey? Where are you?" she says. "We've all been so worried. How are the children? How's your mother doing?"

She got upset when I told her Mama's pregnant.

"He has no business dragging her all over the country. And you kids should be in school. It's outrageous."

The last time she and Daddy talked, she called him a criminal, robbing his children of a home and education. She threatened to report him to the authorities.

That was a mistake. Now he won't let us mention her name. Anyway, there's no one to report us to. We're always moving someplace else.

The wash is done and I stuff it in the dryers. A girl comes in with a little child. His feet are bare and the floor is filthy. He's eating an enormous candy bar.

The girl gets her clothes going then sits down near me. When I glance up, she smiles. She's not much older than I am. Her face is thin and pointy but pretty.

"You new here?" she asks.

"A couple of weeks."

"It's not too bad. They keep the place pretty clean. Want a cigarette?"

"Thanks." My parents don't know I've started smoking. I do it sometimes. I don't know why.

"We've been here about a year," she says. "We're leaving soon. Going to Reno. Ever been there?"

"No."

"My old man's a trucker. He's got something lined up. What's your old man do?"

"He used to sell insurance but now he works at Thrifty."

"That's great. How many kids you got?"

"Well, none, actually."

"Oh, sorry." She laughs. "I seen all the dryers. I guess I jumped to conclusions."

"I've got sisters."

"You got a car? The reason I ask is, I got to get into town. I've got an appointment at Social Services. You been down there yet?"

"No."

"You should. You could get stamps, maybe."

"Stamps?"

"Food stamps. Every little bit helps, that's for sure."

My father would never agree to that. He doesn't believe in taking charity. He says too many people want something for nothing. He says that's what's wrong with this country.

"My dad's got a job now. We'll be okay."

"That's great." She watches her son play with a cigarette butt. "Put that down, Jerry. It's dirty, honey." He stuffs it in his mouth and pretends to puff.

"My old man tried to get work around here, but shoot, the minorities got it all locked up. Don't get me wrong, I'm not prejudiced or nothing, but that's not right. This was our country first." She laughs. "Now I sound just like my old man. You should hear him when he gets started! He can only get back here twice a month. But he thinks he's found a steady thing in Reno. Ever been there?"

"No."

"It's great, all the casinos. My girlfriend's going to get me a job as a change girl. She says they got day care, too. Course, I'm pregnant again but it's not like I show yet. I'm still so skinny. You're pretty skinny, too. How tall are you, anyway?"

"Five nine."

"That's tall for a girl. You're lucky you're not a little shrimp like me. People look down on you, in more ways than one. Can I look at that thing if you're done with it?" She holds out her hand for the real-estate magazine.

I fold the warm clothes. My stomach is growling. There was only dry cereal for breakfast. When Daddy gets his first paycheck, we're going to have a feast. We'll barbecue steaks and have corn on the cob, and apple pie with vanilla ice cream and a wedge of cheddar cheese for Daddy. He says the sharpness of the cheese makes the apples taste extra sweet.

The Jeep's parked outside the RV. It's not supposed to be there. Maybe Daddy came home for lunch. He hasn't done that before, but there's probably some good reason, like maybe he has terrific news. Maybe they've promoted him to manager already. They probably said, "Andrew, we can't afford to lose a man with your experience. So we're giving you a promotion and a big fat raise. And we're starting your medical insurance today so your wife can get a doctor for the baby."

I can hear Daddy shouting from thirty feet away.

Inside, the kids stare at the TV, eyes large with alarm, their faces blank. They try to be invisible when my father's angry.

Bits of sentences spray out of his mouth.

"Thinks he can talk to me like that! Snotnosed kid! Don't have to take that! I told that punk—"

Weeping, my mother clutches her stomach as if she were comforting the child inside.

"Daddy, what's wrong?"

"Get ready. We're leaving."

"Right now? What happened? Did you get fired again?"

The look he gives me is like a blow.

"'Again'? Did I get fired 'again'? Oh, yes, I get fired all the time, don't I?"

"No, but—"

"I used to manage an office! A multimillion-dollar operation! And that punk, that shit, talks to me like that! In front of customers! They were laughing at me!"

I can read the look that Mama gives me. She wants me to ask what she's afraid to ask. When I do, she'll look reproachful, like: Mary, how could you?

"Did you get your money?"

"No, I didn't get my money. Do you think I'm going to crawl back and beg for my paycheck? How much is a man's dignity worth these days, Mary? Two, three hundred dollars a week?"

"But you earned that money!"

"That's right! I earned it. Not you, not your mother. Me! Are you in charge now? Are you running this family?"

"It's your money! We need it!"

"Not one more word!"

"How much is your pride going to cost this family?"

Mama cries, "Andrew, don't!"

He turns to her. "Did you think I was going to hit her, Wendy? Have I ever in my life hit one of my children? Have I ever raised a hand to you? All I'm trying to do is take care of my family. You

24

know that, don't you? Don't you understand, Wendy?"

He collapses beside her. They're hugging and sobbing.

The little girls glare. Not at them; at me.

Erica says, "Mary, you're mean."

My brain feels like it's exploding. I want to scream. I want to slap my parents and shout: *Wake up!*

But my family thinks it's cruel to wake the dreamer from the dream.

So I start packing.

Three

Look at the Wolfs' Den from a distance and you think: That thing must've cost a fortune. It did. Those people must have a lot of money. They don't. Not anymore.

Look closer and see that the skylights leak. Dried puddles stain the ceiling. The fenders are dented, the paint is peeling, the curtains have shattered from the heat of the sun. A crack sneaks relentlessly across the windshield. Eventually it will have to be replaced.

The tires are my big concern right now. The tread's almost gone. That's dangerous; if they blow out, you can lose control. So many cars have lousy tires. I notice tires everywhere we go, in gas stations, parking lots, truck stops.

Yesterday I showed Daddy the right rear radial, where the steel belt's poking through the rubber.

He frowned. "It's just that one tire. The others are fine."

"No they're not. Take a look."

He didn't want to look. "There are thousands of miles left on those tires, Mary. I'll get the back one patched."

"They won't patch it. It's shot."

"Since when did you become an expert on tires?"

Since two years ago, when I started changing them. The first time I helped him, Mama protested, "Andrew, you shouldn't make her do that. That's boy stuff."

"Girls get flat tires, too, Wendy. It wouldn't hurt you to learn to do this. The more you know, the less you have to fear. Remember that, Mary," Daddy said. "Use this wrench."

This morning he and Mama unhitched the Jeep and drove into town to buy some food and pick up a copy of the local paper so Daddy could look through the want ads. We were staying in an RV park in the hills. The town was spread across the valley below. Daddy checked out the park before he signed in. He says you can tell a lot from the bathrooms.

As soon as they left, I turned off the TV.

"I want to watch the Flintstones!" Erica howls.

"Not till we're done studying."

"They'll be over by then!"

"I want Mommy!" Polly says.

"She'll be back."

"Maybe not."

"Knock it off, Danielle," I say. "Don't tease her."

"I'm not. I'm just saying things happen sometimes."

"Something's going to happen to you right now if you don't shut up."

"You're not the boss of me."

"Yes I am. I'm in charge when they're gone. Erica, finish your toast."

"I can't. It's mushy."

"Then throw it away."

"I'm still hungry."

"No you're not. Polly, don't wipe your nose on your arm. Get some toilet paper out of the bathroom."

I clear the table and pass around paper and pencils and give Polly crayons and a coloring book.

"We're going to miss *The Brady Bunch*," Erica mutters.

"*Brady Bunch*!" Polly echoes.

"Listen to me, you girls. One of these days you'll be in school and have to do what the teacher tells you. And you won't get to sit around and watch TV. We'll do some math first. Is everybody ready? Now, pretend Mama has ten dollars and milk is two dollars a gallon. How many gallons can Mama buy?"

How many imaginary loaves of bread? How many tires can you buy with no money? The girls groan and gnaw their pencils.

"Pretend Mama has twenty dollars and she's going to buy some candy."

"What kind?" Erica says.

"I don't know. Tootsie Pops."

"I want Mars bars."

"Pretend she's buying any kind you want! The point is, each bag of candy costs three dollars. How many bags can Mama buy and how much change will she have left?"

"Is there tax?" Danielle asks.

"No."

"I want candy!" Polly says.

"Shut up, you baby."

"Don't tell her to shut up, Danielle. Just do your work."

The refrigerator hums while the girls scribble. The seal is old and should be replaced. Outside, the sky is clogged with clouds. The trailers and RVs look shabby and wet.

Sometimes, when I'm driving, I pretend we're pioneers, crossing the frontier in a Conestoga wagon, heading toward a new life and a homestead of our own, with flowers and fruit trees and a vegetable garden, and a house as firmly rooted as an ancient oak.

I make Danielle and Erica read aloud. Then it's time for their music lesson. I open my guitar case and the girls crowd around as if it were a treasure chest. It is; my guitar is my most precious possession. Aunt Belle gave it to me for my tenth birthday. She taught me how to strum and finger chords.

"Let me play, Mary."

"No, Polly. You're too little."

"No, I'm not. I want to play!"

"Don't be a baby."

"She is a baby, Danielle. Just shut up and sing."

"How can I sing if I shut up?"

"I want to watch *Flipper*," Erica says. "Mama always lets us watch it."

"Well, Mama's not here. Pretty soon you girls will be back in school. Someday you'll have to go to college and get jobs."

"Daddy says there aren't any jobs."

"There are jobs, Erica, it's just hard to find them. But Daddy's smart and he can do it. Now we're going to sing some songs."

"What's the point of singing songs? You can't get a job singing."

"Yes you can, Danielle. There's lots of famous singers. Some people sing in the opera."

"I hate that stuff. La la la la la!"

"Who cares?" I say. "Who cares about the opera? Maybe you'll deliver singing telegrams!

30

The point is, you can't live in an RV all your life. There are so many things you need to know."

And so many things I can't teach them. They don't understand that they won't always be kids. Tomorrow's someplace they've never been.

I play songs for the girls and they sing along. I show them how to gently pluck the strings. The guitar speaks for me. It's my heart singing. Daddy always says, "Why's it sound so sad?"

I replace the strings regularly; the best middle-weight gauge. I do what it takes to get them. Beg money from Mama. Sell aluminum cans. It takes so many to make a pound. Mama says put a pebble in each one to weigh it down but Daddy says no, that's cheating. Mama says, "Andrew, you know they cheat us! You know they're taking our money!"

I love all kinds of music; blues and country and rock. You can get tapes cheap, used or bootleg, at flea markets. When I drive the RV, I command the tape deck. I do most of the driving lately; Daddy's stomach's been bothering him. I crank up the volume and play along, accompanying the band on my invisible guitar; onstage, ripping out a riff. A star. Until Daddy says, "Turn that down."

"Okay," I tell the girls, "now you're going to write a story."

"A story!" Danielle snorts. "I don't even like to read."

"Well, you better like to read, because you're going to be doing a lot of it."

"No I'm not. I hate books."

"What about signs? Like signs on the freeway? What about *TV Guide*? You want to know when the Flintstones are on, don't you?"

"I want to watch the Flintstones," Erica whines.

"Not till we're done. Now pick up your pencils. Not you, Polly. You can color in your book."

"I want to write, too!"

"Okay, here's some paper."

"Oh boy, I can't wait to read her story."

"Danielle, will you give me a break? You're really being a jerk today."

"Look who's talking. You think you're so big."

"Don't be rude," Erica says, "or I'll tell Daddy."

"Tattletale. Blabbermouth."

"Everybody shut up!"

"Don't say *shut up*, Mary. That's not nice."

"Polly, will you please—just put away your crayons."

"I can't. There's too many. Will you help me, Mary?"

"Yes. But you start."

"Then can I watch TV?"

"In a while. Okay, here's the opening sentence: 'When I was a little girl, I left home on a big trip.' Take it from there."

"Take it where?" Danielle says.

"Wherever you want. That's just the beginning."

"It's boring."

"Then make it interesting! Write whatever you want!"

"Does it have to be long?"

"No. But make it neat. I want to be able to read it."

Erica writes: "When I was a little girl I left home on a big trip. We saw Mickey Mouse. Mama's having a baby."

Danielle scrawls: "When I was a little girl I left home on a big trip. At first it was fun seeing all the different places. Now everywhere we go looks like this goddam trailer park."

"That's great Danielle. That's swell."

"You said I could write whatever I want." She crumples up the paper and turns on the TV. Erica and Polly draw close to the flickering screen, as if it were a cozy fire.

Danielle knows we're going nowhere, that we're driving in circles. She remembers how life used to be, back home. A house without wheels. A yard of our own. Erica and Polly were little; their memories are hazy. Daddy loves to tell them stories about the old days. He makes our house sound like a fairytale castle; countless rooms, closets bulging with clothes, fluffy towels in gleaming bathrooms, a row of shiny bikes, a swing set and slide, a wide lawn swept with melting diamonds and the laughter of children playing in the sprinkler, the sun above us like a big white smile, shining down upon our family.

Daddy and Mama tell the girls we'll move back there someday.

They don't know I know the house is gone.

I heard them talking one night when they thought I was asleep.

"You sold it?" she repeated. "What do you mean, you sold it?"

"I sold it. It's gone. Aren't you listening to me?"

"You're lying," Mama whispered fiercely. "You couldn't sell the house without my signature!"

He said, "Where'd you think all the money was coming from?"

"I don't know! We had money in the savings. We had money in the savings! That's what you said."

"I made some investments. Things didn't pan out."

His voice was flat. She asked no more questions. I lay in the dark, listening to Mama weep.

Daddy and Mama return, bearing sacks of groceries and a white paper bag from the bakery.

"Did you bring me something?" Polly leaps at the bag. Mama kisses her and hands her a cookie.

"I got hired at the furniture factory," Daddy announces. "They make picnic tables and lawn chairs. I can do that in my sleep. The pay's not great but it's a start."

"You'll be running the place in a week," Mama says, cupping her hands under her big belly.

"We checked out the schools. They look good," he says. "You girls can start tomorrow."

"Do we have to?"

"Of course you have to, Danielle," he tells her sternly. "It's against the law for children to be dumb." He winks to show he's kidding. She smiles uncertainly. "After lunch we'll drive down and look around. I'm sure you girls are curious about your new town."

Erica snuggles on his lap. "What's it called, Daddy?"

He has to think for a moment. There have been so many towns.

"Cloverdale. It's a pretty little place. I think we're going to like it here. And Mary, you'll be pleased to know we've ordered new tires. A complete set. Are you happy now?"

I say, "It's like a dream come true."

Four

I thought Daddy would drive us to school the first day, but he said we should take the bus.

"It will pick you up at the bottom of the hill. You can make new friends right away," he said.

Erica shrank. She's shy with strangers. "I want you to take us, Daddy," she whimpered.

"You heard your father. Get dressed," Mama said. "The bus will be here at seven thirty."

My parents usually act like they can't breathe without us. Other times, we seem to suffocate them. It's strange.

Safely nestled in their bed, Polly watched us get dressed. "I can't tie my shoes," Erica cried. I helped her. Then we gulped down our breakfast and left the RV, the fog enveloping the girls' bare legs. California's supposed to be warm, the climate kind to migrating birds and people.

Over Mama's objections I'd worn my jeans.

She thinks girls look more feminine in dresses. You don't want to stick out in a new school. No Kick Me signs. Jeans are pretty generic.

Most of the time I don't see my sisters clearly. They're too close for me to be objective. At the bus stop the girls come into focus. Framed in space, they look out-of-place, lost.

Danielle stamps her feet.

"You should've worn your coat," I tell her.

"I hate that coat. I'm not cold," she snarls. When Danielle's scared, she acts mad, instead. She got into fights at the last school she attended.

"Don't worry, you look fine."

She rolls her eyes. Most of our clothes come from yard sales and thrift shops. Her dress is too short and her sweater's too big. She bangs her lunch bag against her legs.

"I don't see why he couldn't give us a ride," she says. "It's not like he was doing anything."

"He has to have a physical for his job today."

"Not till later."

"Maybe his stomach was bothering him."

"His stomach's always bothering him," she mutters, chucking a rock into the vineyard across the road.

"Don't worry, I'll take you to school this morning."

"I can do it myself," she protests, relieved.

"Me too, Mary?" Erica clutches my hand. She looks so little in her blue plaid dress, her blond hair twisted into shiny braids. Danielle's hair was long until she hacked it off with scissors. Mama had a fit.

"You too, hon. It will be all right. You'll love being in school again. Wait and see."

"I can wait," Danielle says. Erica huddles beside me. She'd climb inside my pocket if she fit.

The bus looms out of the fog and groans to a stop. The door swings open and the driver greets us.

"Good morning, girls," she says. "There's seats in back."

I shove the girls up the steps and down the aisle, through a tunnel of goggle-eyed faces. We find seats together. Erica sits on my lap. She'd suck her thumb if kids weren't watching.

We pass farmhouses, barns, and misty vineyards, and ghostly oak trees draped with moss. We cross a bridge over the river and drive downtown, past beauty shops, markets, gas stations, the post office, the high school, to the grade school at the north end of town.

I get off with the girls. I'll walk to the high school. Mama and Daddy registered the girls yesterday, but we need to find out the location of their rooms.

The secretary gives us directions, then says, "Remind your parents that we'll need the girls' transcripts for our records."

"They'll be here soon," I promise. There are no transcripts. We've been everywhere and nowhere. And won't be here long enough for it to matter.

In the first-grade wing we meet Erica's teacher. Mrs. Donatelli kneels down and smiles at Erica, and shows her where to put her lunch bag and coat. Erica's pleased to have the teacher's attention, but when I move toward the door, she says, "Mary, don't go."

"I have to, honey. I'll meet you out front, after school."

"She'll be fine," the teacher says. "We'll have lots of fun."

"That's what they all say," Danielle grumbles. We head down the hall to her fourth-grade classroom.

"I should be in fifth grade. I was last time."

"Yeah, but you never caught up. Now you'll probably be the smartest kid in your class."

"Oh goody," she says, looking miserable.

Her classroom is empty. Her teacher's on the playground, supervising the kids before the final bell rings. I introduce my sister. He greets her warmly and says, "So tell me, Danielle, where did you live before this?"

"I'll see you after school," I say. She shrugs.

I walk quickly toward the high school. It's an old brick building surrounded by portable classrooms. I'm glad I wore jeans; most of the girls wear pants. Class hasn't started; kids are milling around or standing in little groups. Radar tingling, they sense me immediately. I move through a restless sea of whispers.

In the office a bunch of girls who cut class are giving the secretary a dramatic excuse. "Well, that's just thrilling," she says when they're through. They shriek their innocence while checking me out, quickly dismissing me as competition. Not ugly or beautiful, just there, like air. Invisibility is the look I'm after.

The school counselor gives me my locker combination and tells me to see him if I have any problems.

I won't. My parents don't like problems, don't like coming to school for meetings. There are too many questions they can't answer. They're ashamed to explain that we live in our RV. In big cities there are lots of homeless people, but in little towns you feel like a freak. So I'm friendly and polite, but I keep my distance. It makes saying good-bye easier.

The bell rings and I go to my English class. The room is crammed; a custodian hauls in my desk and sets it in back by the door. The teacher gives me a copy of *Moby Dick*. I've studied it twice before.

The girl across the aisle catches my eye and smiles, so I smile back, then look at my book. At a new school, you don't know what's what or who's who. Lots of lonely people glom onto the new kid and try to make you their instant best friend. Sometimes they're lonely because they're so nice, and sometimes because they're crazy. Like this girl Eileen I met in Missouri. She invited me to spend the night the very first day. She said the kids hated her; that they were really mean. But she was mean, too, in her own way; she was bossy and asked a lot of personal questions. I felt like she was trying to crawl inside my brain and read my mind. I wasn't sorry when we moved away.

After English, I had history, home ec, and PE. I didn't have gym clothes, so I sat on the bench and watched the girls play softball, crashing into each other and screaming with laughter when they thought any boys were looking.

The worst times at a new school are breaks and lunch. You can get through breaks by hanging out in the bathroom and combing your hair. Lunchtime is awful. It's way too long. I walk around eating, trying to look busy. Some schools have areas that are off-limits. At one school I was eating lunch in a deserted courtyard and two girls came by and said, "You can't be here. You're not a senior." They waited till I left, then they left, too.

I go to my locker and pretend to arrange it. The girl from my English class instantly materializes, as if she's been lurking nearby.

"Hi," she says. "I'm in your English class, remember?"

"Yes." I smile, then glance into my locker as if it commands my attention.

"So how do you like the school so far?"

"It's okay," I say. "I haven't been here very long."

"I know. I saw you in the office this morning. Where do you live?"

"In the hills," I answer vaguely.

"Where'd you live before this?"

"Oh, different places."

"Like where? Have you ever been to Redding? That's where my dad lives. I wish we could move there. The people there are really nice. But my mother's got this boyfriend and he lives here." The girl made a face. "Oh. My name is Beth. I forgot to tell you."

"I'm Mary."

"Your hair's so long. Has it always been like that?"

"Not when I was born."

The joke clears her head. "I mean since you were big."

"Yeah, I guess."

"It might look better short. I mean, no offense. It's just that nobody wears their hair like that. I mean, you can if you want. It looks real pretty."

"Thanks." I plow through my purse as though I'm hunting for something crucial; my class schedule, the meaning of life, the key to the car that will drive me away.

"So do you want to eat lunch together tomorrow?"

"Maybe," I say. "I might be busy."

"Doing what?"

"I might have to see a teacher or something. You know, to catch up on my assignments."

"It must be hard to be new in school and not know anybody. I know everybody here. We've been together since kindergarten. It's nice, you know, but it's kind of disgusting. I mean, you get tired of the same old faces. That's why I want to move away."

"It's nice to meet new people," I say. "Well, there's the bell. See you tomorrow."

After lunch I have science and math. This math class is way ahead of me. The teacher suggests that I come in after school for extra help.

"I have to pick up my sisters after school. How about lunchtime tomorrow?" I suggest.

All across the country, schools are pretty much alike. The sameness is a comfort, in a way. It's like going to Howard Johnson's; you can count on getting pancakes. No flaming shish kabobs, no singing waiters. Bored kids, worn-out books, tired teachers trying hard.

Some schools have more money than others. There are plenty of books and supplies and field trips, and the classrooms aren't so crowded. At one school I went to in Colorado, most of the kids had their own cars.

This school's in the middle, not rich or poor. I wouldn't mind staying until graduation. If I do, people will think I'm nice but most of them will never know my name. You know who I mean; the new girl, they'll say. In my yearbook they'll write: *To a great kid*. I would like to be in a yearbook someday. I would like to go to a class reunion.

After my last class I hurry to the grade school. Hundreds of kids swarm around the buses. Erica waves a handful of papers in my face. "Mary, look what I did in school!"

Our bus is loading up but Danielle won't get on. She's got her arms crossed, fists stuffed into her armpits, and that stubborn-as-cement look on her face.

"Come on. What's the problem? The bus is leaving."

"You can leave if you want. I'm walking."

"You can't walk home, Danielle. It's too far." But she turns her back and stalks down the side-walk.

"It's okay," I tell the driver. "I guess we'll walk."

I grab Erica's hand and we catch up with Danielle. Her angry eyes are glittering with tears.

"What's the matter? What's the problem?" She just keeps walking until I grab her arm and make her stop.

"We're not going anywhere till you tell me what's wrong."

"Mary!" Erica wails. "There goes the bus! Now we'll never get home!"

"Yes we will. What's wrong, Danielle? Did something happen at school?"

"Just leave me alone!" She swings at me. I catch her fist and hold her tight.

"Quit acting like that! Did you get into a fight?"

"No, but I will! They know where we live!"

"What are you talking about?"

"They laughed!"

"Who laughed?"

"This boy! He lives in one of those big houses on the way to the campground. He told everyone we're poor. I'll kill him. I hate him! And I'm not going to bring my lunch anymore! They all bought lunch in the cafeteria! I'm not eating any lunch! I'm never going back there!"

I try to hug her but she pulls away.

"Why do we have to be different?" she says. "Why can't we just be the same?"

"Someday we will be." Now Erica is crying. I fish a tissue from my purse and wipe her nose. "Listen to me, Danielle. Lots of people don't have money these days. That's how it is. But things are getting better. Daddy's working now and pretty soon we'll rent a house. Maybe you can have your own room."

"Me too," Erica says. "But I might get lonely."

"You don't need to feel ashamed because you can't buy lunch."

"I'm not bringing any lunch! I'd rather starve!"

She tries to act tough, but she's just a kid. Maybe this school has a free-lunch program. If Daddy won't sign up, I'll pay for it myself. It won't cost much. I'll get a job after school. It's time I was bringing in some money.

"Come on," I tell the girls. "We've got a long walk home."

Erica says, "Maybe Daddy could come and get us."

"Duhhh, we don't have a phone," Danielle says.

"We can walk," I say. "It's not going to kill us. But tomorrow we're taking the bus, Danielle. And you're not going to fight with that kid. Ignore him.

"I'm going to punch out his lights."

"Then I'll punch out yours."

"Go ahead and try."

"Do you hear me? Ignore him."

We walk past a store that sells baked goods and ice cream. A sweet-smelling breeze reaches through the screen door. I look in my wallet. New guitar strings can wait.

"Who wants an ice cream cone?"

"Me!" Erica claps her hands.

"Me," Danielle says. "I'm starving."

Five

We haven't been able to move into a house yet.
Some people won't rent to a big family. Rents are
high and you have to have first and last months'
rent, a security deposit, and money to turn on
the gas and electric. We'll need to save up at least
two thousand dollars. Meanwhile, there's food
and gas and other expenses. It's amazing how
much life costs.

Every night Daddy comes home from work
covered with sawdust and heads for the campground showers, first thing. The RV's shower is
too small for him and Mama, with her big belly
now, to turn around in. Then, at supper, he com-
plains about his job. He says the manager is a big
jerk who doesn't know his ass from his elbow.

"It's incredible they've stayed in business
this long. He's running the place into the ground.
I mean it. I said to him, 'George, are you trying

to make money or using this place for a tax write-off?'"

Mama says, "Andrew, don't make him mad." She's afraid he'll lose his job.

"Are you there, Wendy? Have you seen what's going on? Don't you believe what I'm telling you?"

She stares at her plate. "Of course I do. It's just that they've been in business since—"

"Nineteen sixty-three. Yes, I told you that. But times change, and you have to change with the times. Do you have any idea how many companies have gone belly up this year? And it's not because they weren't making a good product. I've tried to tell George. He's not listening to me. He thinks I'm some bum from the street. Christ, I had twelve guys working under me and now I can't go to the john without permission."

The girls eat quickly so they can watch TV. Danielle claims she does her homework at school. I've told Mama she should talk to Danielle's teacher.

"Daddy works all day. I have no way to get there."

"You could call her on the phone by the laundry room."

"I've tried that," Mama told me. "I can never get through."

Anyway, Danielle's her daughter, not mine.

School's okay. People leave me alone. The

teachers are helping me catch up. On Saturdays and Sundays I wash dishes at the truck stop. The waitresses give me food to bring home. I keep ten dollars a week and give the rest to Mama, who banks it in an old cloth purse.

I thought my parents would be pleased about the job, but Daddy hates taking my money and Mama misses my help. She doesn't make the girls do anything. When I get home from work, the RV's a mess, dirty dishes and clothes piled everywhere, the girls and Mama in bed, watching TV. "Feel, Mary." She'll place my hand on her rolling belly. "That's the baby's little elbow or knee."

Unless it's the news or an educational program, TV annoys my father. After supper he reads the newspapers, calling my attention to every bankruptcy, every mass layoff, every fresh financial disaster.

"Look at this." He'll whack the business section. "Look at this, Mary. You want to tell me why anyone needs to make sixty million dollars a year? Plus benefits? Is that kind of money really necessary?"

"No," I'll say. "It seems insane."

"How much do you think the little guys are getting; the guys who deliver all those cans of beer that are paying this joker's salary? Without the little guys it would all grind to a halt, but they're so stupid they don't even know that."

Who's so stupid? The big guys or the little

guys? My father's fall has altered his perspective.

The baby's due soon and Daddy's been trying to find a doctor for Mama, but none of the doctors in town will take us until his medical insurance begins. That won't be for two more months, until he's passed probation.

Daddy figures we'll drive to the hospital in Healdsburg when Mama's in labor. The people in the emergency room will probably refuse to take her, because we don't have insurance or money. Then Daddy will triumph in his righteous wrath.

"No, you won't take us," he plans to shout, "but you'll take all those welfare patients! Half of them aren't even citizens of this country! Go ahead and turn us away! I'll sue this hospital from hell to Sunday if anything happens to my wife or baby!"

I've begged them to apply for Medi-Cal benefits.

Absolutely not, Daddy says. We're no welfare cheats, no deadbeats scheming to get something for nothing.

"But Mama should see a doctor!"

She laughs at me. "For heaven's sake, Mary. I'm going to have a baby, not a heart attack. You worry too much."

I wouldn't, if she'd worry more.

When we come in after school, Mama's lying on her bed.

"Mary," she says. Her face looks strained.

"What's the matter, Mama? Are you all right?"

"I think it's time."

I drop my books. "Are you sure?"

"Honey, this is my fifth baby. I guess I recognize the signs by now. Whew, this place is like an oven!"

The little girls are wide-eyed. "Nothing's wrong," I tell them, opening doors and windows. "The baby's on its way, that's all."

I fix them a snack and turn on the cartoons. The girls watch Mama from the corners of their eyes.

"We should call Daddy."

"He'll be home soon. There's time."

"How long has this been going on?"

"All afternoon."

"Polly came fast," I remind her. "Does it hurt?"

She's wincing. "A little. But it's a good hurt, Mary. Someday you'll know what I mean."

Maybe. I'm not sure I'll have babies. It seems like I've had children all my life. "Are you sure you're all right?"

"I'm fine. Just hot." She catches her breath, her eyes squeeze shut. When she opens them, they shine with tears.

"Mary, bring me some water. With ice. I'm so thirsty."

I consider calling Daddy, but he's already left

work. I hope he comes right home; her last labor was short. She's proud of the way babies pop out of her.

By tomorrow afternoon she'll be home with the new baby. If it's a girl, Mama wants to call her Amy, but Daddy's leaning toward Roberta. He lets Mama choose our middle names.

I give Mama the ice water. She can't get comfortable. She pants and rubs ice cubes on her neck and wrists.

"Mama, maybe you should get up and walk around. You might feel better."

"Maybe you're right." But when she stands up, water pours down her legs.

"Mama peed!" Erica giggles nervously. But it's not pee; the sac that holds the baby has ruptured. This baby is on its way.

"Mama, we should go to the hospital now. I'll leave a note for Daddy." But we can't just go; the tables must be folded, the awning must be rolled up, everything must be secured before the RV can be driven. "I'm going to call the ambulance."

"No," she gasps, then pain grips her. It's coming in waves now, sharp and fast. "He'll be home any second. I won't leave without Daddy."

Polly wants me to hold her. I pick her up, then place her on Danielle's lap. Erica sucks her thumb so hard I can hear her. Mama rubs her belly and groans.

"Everything's fine," I tell the girls. "Nothing's wrong, nothing's the matter. As soon as Daddy gets here, he'll take Mama to the hospital and then she'll have the baby. Won't that be nice?"

"I don't want Mommy to go to the hospital!" Polly wails. Erica's crying, too. Danielle's eyes are dry and bitter.

I stroke Mama's forehead and tell her to relax while she pants through the pains, her face glistening with sweat. It seems like forever before we hear the Jeep chugging up the hill.

I rush outside. Daddy slams the Jeep's door. "You know what that bastard did?" he announces. "Said he was going to dock my pay! I told that idiot—"

"Daddy," I begin, but I can't reach him. I can't scale the wall of my father's rage.

"They give them to the employees! Free! Those mill ends were mine! We can't use them in the RV so I sold them. So what? I told that bastard—"

"Daddy, listen to me. Mama's having the baby."

"What?" he says. "Really?" He runs inside.

The girls are frozen. Mama's moaning and twisting.

"Wendy, darling." He strokes her hair. "Daddy's here. It will be all right."

"It's coming too fast. Oh, God, it hurts!"

Mama screams. The girls are sobbing.

I tell them to calm down, to watch TV. Bugs Bunny is blaring in the background. "Mama's fine," I say. What if something is wrong? What if Mama and the baby are dying?

"I think we should call 911," I tell Daddy.

"I can take her in the Jeep."

"There's not time! Can't you see that?"

"What's wrong?" Danielle cries.

"Nothing's wrong," I say. "Mama's just having the baby."

"I've got to push!" she shouts.

"Try to wait, Mama, please. We're going to get the ambulance," I tell her. Daddy's wringing his hands, tears stream down his cheeks. "Daddy, will you please go call them?"

"No!" Mama screams. "Andrew, don't leave me!"

"I'll never leave you, Wendy. I'm right here."

"I'll go call." I start for the door.

"I've got to push! I can't wait! It hurts! Where's Mary?"

"Mary!" Daddy shouts. "She needs you! Come here!"

I stroke Mama's face. Her head whips from side to side.

"Something's wrong. I can feel it. The baby's dropped down," she gasps. "Mary, something's wrong with the baby!"

I shove Daddy toward the door. "Call the

ambulance! Now! Take the girls. Get them out of here!" They follow him, wailing.

"Someone help me!" Mama cries. "Please help me! It hurts!"

I kneel by her side. "You'll be fine, Mama. Really. This baby's in a hurry to be born, that's all. Now take some deep breaths and try to relax."

When babies are born on TV, people always boil water. I boil water in the microwave. What do I do with it now?

"Mary, it's so— Oh, God, I'm dying!"

"No you're not, Mama. You're doing fine. The ambulance is on its way. Before you know it, you'll be holding the baby. Lie still and let me look at you. Lie still!"

I push up her nightgown and spread her legs, afraid of what I'm going to see. A demon infant, tearing Mama apart. Or a tiny foot stepping into the world, the baby turned the wrong way around.

Mama's thighs are smeared with blood. A tiny patch of scalp bulges at the opening between her legs, then recedes.

I bathe her with the water and spread towels beneath her hips. I pray to God: Please, please don't let my mother die. Please let the baby be all right.

Mama's writhing and panting. "Mary, we've got to get out of here! I can't do this anymore! We've got to leave!"

"You're doing fine, Mama. The baby will be here any second."

"I've got to push!" she screams. "Oh, Mary, it's coming!"

She tears wide open, the baby's head pops out, covered with blood and white stuff.

"Push, Mama. Push!"

Slick shoulders slide through, then the baby glides onto the bed between her thighs, followed by a pulsing purple cord.

I pick up the baby. He's wet and slippery. His nose is plugged. I wipe it clean. I rub him with a towel and pat his back until he cries; a piping shriek, and then an outraged squall.

Released from pain, Mama's face is exhausted, exalted, delighted.

"Look at him, Mary! He's so beautiful," she croons, "the most beautiful little baby I've ever seen."

I wrap him in a blanket and place him on her breast, draping the thick cord across her belly. She unbuttons her nightgown and his tiny red face turns blindly toward her warmth.

Daddy bursts through the door. "The ambulance is coming!"

"Andrew," Mama says, "come and meet your son."

He tiptoes inside, the girls trailing behind him. I've never seen that expression on his face. It's joy. And I realize that my sisters were supposed to be boys, the son he's waited for all along, time after time, Daniel, Eric, and Paul.

My father's dream has finally been born.

"A boy! A boy." Daddy kneels beside the bed, touching my brother's scrunched-up face, his hair.

"What's that snaky thing?" Erica points.

"It's the cord. It helped the baby breathe inside Mama," I explain. "They'll cut it when we get to the hospital."

"There's no need to go to the hospital. Everything's fine now," Daddy says.

"Doctors should check them out, to be sure."

"There's nothing wrong with this boy. Look at him nurse!" Daddy says proudly, his head resting on Mama's shoulder.

"What'll we call him?" Mama's smiling, stroking Daddy's hair. "We never expected a boy."

She's wrong.

"Andrew Michael Wolf, Junior," my father murmurs. "Andy for short."

Six

Daddy told his boss that he didn't mean to call him an idiot and he'd be willing to take his job back, no hard feelings, but George said no.

So he found a job at a gas station in town. The hours were crummy; he worked all night, but he said he got a lot of thinking done, with no one there to bug him.

It was hard for him to sleep during the day; May was warm and the RV got hot. Also, Andy was crying a lot. Mama thought he might have colic. We'd hold him and rock him and Mama would nurse him, but he'd draw up his little legs and holler.

Erica and Polly could shut out the noise, but Andy really got to Danielle.

"Why's he do that all the time?" she'd whine. "Can't we put a pillow over his face?"

She's jealous because he's Daddy's favorite. That's how it is with a new baby. They're the littlest and cutest and everybody loves them. Daddy's especially proud of Andy, as if this boy is himself reborn.

Doting on Andy doesn't mean Daddy takes care of him. He believes that's the mother's job. Once, he proudly told Aunt Belle, "I've never changed a diaper."

"What kind of father are you?" she asked, appalled.

"The kind that hates dirty diapers." He'd grinned.

Mama takes care of Andy when she can, but she's tired. Mostly she nurses him and I do the rest. I bathe him in the sink, cradling his tender head. His eyes never leave my face. He kicks and splashes and makes us laugh. Then I dress him in the soft cotton T-shirts that were Polly's, and a disposable diaper. They're expensive, but Mama says cloth ones would give him a rash.

I'm surprised how much I love him; he's a lot of work. But that's his job, he's a baby. He didn't appoint himself the little king. Daddy anointed him and gave him his crown.

It's warm, I've got the windows open, driving to my next engagement, a sold-out concert in a famous hall. My fans are fighting over tickets.

Daddy says, "Mary, turn that down."

"It's pretty, Daddy. You'll love it. Just listen."

"And put out that cigarette. You have no

business smoking. It's a disgusting habit."

"You're right, Daddy. I plan to quit."

"You stop right now, do you hear me, Mary?"

But I don't stop, and he doesn't make me. He closes the screen between the cab and the rest of the RV. I turn up the tape. k.d. lang is singing, her voice pure and clean. I pretend it's me. It's a gorgeous day, a perfect day for driving, even though I don't know where I'm going.

I was sorry to leave Cloverdale. The teachers helped me. My English teacher, Mrs. Wilson, loved this story I'd written.

It was about a girl whose family had to move across the country. They had a dog named Rex, he was ten years old. They'd had him since the girl was a baby. The parents said they couldn't take the dog along, so the girl said she wasn't moving either.

When she came home from school the next day, the dog was gone. Her mother said her father had taken Rex to a farm, and that he'd be real happy there, with lots of room to run around. She made it sound like a wonderful place. The girl wished she could live there, too.

That night the girl heard her parents talking and learned that her father had taken Rex to the pound, and that he'd probably be put to sleep, since he was old. "At least he won't suffer," the girl's mother said.

Then the girl had to pretend she didn't know the truth, because that would make her parents liars and killers. And they couldn't be; they were her parents, she loved them.

Mrs. Wilson said it was a wonderful story and submitted it to the school literary magazine. She said she'd send me a copy when it was published. I gave her Aunt Belle's address.

I sent a letter to Aunt Belle, telling her about Andy. "He's a month old now and he's so cute!" I wrote. "And he loves it when I sing so he MUST be a genius! Maybe we'll come back so you can see him."

My father doesn't know about the letter. He called my grandparents when Andy was born and I think he asked them to send us money, because suddenly we had a lot. We got new clothes and a bunch of schoolbooks, and Daddy had some work done on the Jeep but it's still not running right. I asked him to put new tires on it but Daddy says there's nothing wrong with those tires, and besides, what difference does it make; we're towing it, not driving it.

Last night we were heading toward a state park. It took longer to get there than we expected. I drove through the dark, down a winding road, the fog wrapped around the RV like a blindfold.

When we got to the campground there was a chain across the entrance, and my father got out and said, "What the hell?" The fog had lifted and in the headlights we could see that there had been a bad fire and the campground was closed.

The trees were scorched and bare.

We were too tired to keep driving, so we camped for the night. Andy cried a lot. Daddy's stomach hurt. "Can't you do something about that baby?" he said. Mama jiggled Andy and patted his back, but she was frantic; he got more upset.

I wrapped him in a blanket and took him outside and we walked around and around the RV. He stopped crying and turned up his face to the sky.

"Those are stars, Andy," I whispered. "They're really far away. If you knew how far away they are, you wouldn't believe it."

When we went back inside, my father and the girls were sleeping. Mama nursed Andy and put him in his laundry-basket bed.

"Thank you, Mary," she whispered. "You're such a help."

"It's not your fault Andy cries. Daddy shouldn't get mad at you."

"He doesn't mean to. He's just got so much on his mind."

"Who doesn't?"

"Things will be better soon."

"When?"

"Soon," she said firmly. "Let's not wake up the girls."

"I'm not waking up the girls. I just want to talk to you, Mama. We never get to talk. There's always people around."

"Not people," she said. "Your family."

"What's going to happen to us? We can't keep driving around."

"We won't. We just haven't found the right place to settle down yet."

"And we never will, thanks to Daddy. Everywhere we go, he gets in a fight, or something happens and he gets mad and quits. I know why we had to leave Cloverdale. I know what really happened at the gas station."

"I don't know what you mean. Keep your voice down, Mary."

"He stole those parts. They didn't give them to Daddy. He was putting gas in the Jeep without paying."

"That's not true! Those parts were used. They were just going to throw them away! Anyway, so what if he took a little gas? That man hardly paid Daddy anything."

"That doesn't make it right. I don't understand what's happening here. Why is everybody changing? Back home he wouldn't let us take one peanut out of the grocery store. He said that was stealing."

"It was. It is." Mama's face looked tired and heavy. "Mary, you don't understand how hard this is for Daddy. Losing that company just about killed him. He ran that office. That was his office, Mary. Your father was an important man. Now he feels like a failure, a loser, like he can't even feed his own family."

"He can't."

"Do you know how hard that is for a man like Daddy? The last thing he needs is to feel like you don't love him."

"I do love him."

"Or trust him. He's your father, Mary. He's still the head of this family."

"But why does he get to decide what's right? I mean, look at us, Mama. We're camped in a graveyard."

"How was he supposed to know there'd been a fire?"

"He's not. The point is, we shouldn't even be here. We should be in Nebraska, in our beds, sleeping. He would've found another job. But he just, he didn't— Please don't cry, Mama. Please don't cry."

"Oh, Mary," she sighed, leaning her head against my shoulder, "I wish we could go home."

We could leave right now. I'd drive all night, heading toward the dawn and our family in Nebraska. But between us is the country of my father's pride. He'll never go back in disgrace. He'd rather die.

"It's all right, Mama." I patted her shoulder. "Everything will be all right."

I like driving, riding up front alone. I feel powerful, sitting up so high, looking down at the cars whizzing by on the road. The sun keeps snagging on the crack in the windshield, shooting tiny sparks into my eyes.

I grind out my cigarette and turn on the dashboard fan. Why did I start smoking? I keep hoping it will make me feel less tense, but it's just one more thing that makes no sense.

I turn down k.d. lang and push open the screen that separates me from the family.

"We've got to make a decision here soon. Which way do you want to go?"

I've interrupted Daddy at his crossword puzzle. He frowns in the rearview mirror. "I thought we were going to the coast," he says.

"Why? There's no work there."

"You let me worry about that."

"I'm talking about myself. I want to get another job."

There's something my parents don't know about me. I earned more money than I told them about, hiding it in my guitar case; saving it for something, I don't know what. An emergency. A bus ticket.

How could I think of leaving them? It makes me feel like a traitor.

"I don't want you working anymore," Daddy says. "Mama needs your help at home."

"But we need the money. I can help with groceries."

"I don't expect my children to support me. Not until my old age, and I've still got a few good years left." Daddy's mouth is smiling but his eyes are cold. "You just worry about doing well in school."

"There aren't too many schools on the coast. We'd be better off going to the city."

"I'd rather go to the beach," Mama says mildly. She's knitting a cap for Andy's bald head.

"Mama, we're not on vacation," I say.

"We're not?" Daddy looks surprised. "Why didn't somebody tell me?"

He and Mama and the girls giggle, except for Danielle, who stares out the window.

"I think we ought to head over to San Francisco or Oakland," I say. "There's lots more going on over there, and we can always find a place for the RV."

"No," Daddy says. "No more big cities. There's too much crime. And all those people on the street."

"Homeless people, you mean. Like us."

"They're not like us! What's the matter with you?" Daddy throws down his puzzle. "I don't know what's gotten into you lately. You're acting like some bratty teenager. I won't put up with that attitude. Do you hear me, Mary? As far as I'm concerned, there's no such thing as teenagers. Not in this RV. You're either a child or an adult."

Wondering which one that makes me, I take the Highway 1 exit toward the coast.

Seven

We camped on the coast near the town of Mendocino, which was full of beautiful Victorian houses converted into inns and shops. Mama loved it there. We spent one whole morning browsing. Daddy bought Mama a pretty scarf, and a handmade candle in the shape of a whale. Mama let the girls pick out something in the toy store. Erica and Polly got baby dolls. Danielle chose a Chinese kite. In the bookstore Mama offered to buy me a book about the lives of women rock stars. I said no, it cost too much. She surprised me with it at lunch.

The café was downtown, overlooking the ocean. We sat by a window, in the sun. The sea and the sky were as blue as Andy's eyes. The table was decorated with a bouquet of wildflowers.

"This is living." Daddy sighs, sipping his cappuccino. "I mean, look at that view. That's heaven. What do you say we call this place home for a while?"

"This restaurant, you mean?" Mama's smiling.

"You know exactly what I mean, young lady. I can picture you living here, in one of those big houses on the hill. With a porch all around it and a flower garden, no bloom as radiant as you." Daddy raises her hand and kisses it.

The girls have fancy hamburgers and creamy milkshakes that hollow their cheeks and choke their straws. Andy wriggles on Mama's lap, smiling. We do funny stuff to make him laugh, except for Danielle, who ignores him.

"I could get used to a place like this," Daddy says. "I wonder what the rentals go for." He goes outside to a rack and brings back a local paper. He scans the ads, then fans himself, pretending to feel faint. "For these prices, you should own the houses!"

"We could probably find something cheaper," Mama says. "It takes a while. You have to look."

There's a high school in town; we drove past it. If we stayed long enough, I could graduate. But aside from shops and restaurants, there doesn't seem to be much work. It would be hard to make a living here.

"It's too expensive," I say. "We can't afford it."

"Thank you, Mr. Scrooge. Your objection has been noted."

"You never know until you try," Mama says. "Anyway, we could stay in the campground until we save some money."

"Doing what? The help-wanted section is only three inches long."

My father's too content to feel annoyed. He leans across the table and tugs my braid, saying, "How can such a pretty girl look so grumpy?"

I finish my pasta and have chocolate mousse, wondering how we'll pay for this feast. My parents never say how much money they have. Some mornings Mama's stealing Pop Tarts for breakfast but later we'll go out to eat, so it's hard to figure.

I sneak a peek at the bill and review our options: Daddy could write a bad check. He could try to pass one of our expired credit cards. Or he could get up as if he were going to the bathroom, then casually step out the front door, followed by Mama and Andy, then the girls and me. We've done that before.

He surprises me. He produces another thick wad of bills and pays cash, leaving a generous tip for the waitress. Polly hands it back to him. "You forgot this, Daddy."

"No, honey." He and Mama laugh. "We're leaving that here."

We stroll along the sidewalk, Daddy and Mama holding hands, Andy squirming in my arms, trying to watch the traffic.

I say, "Daddy, have you noticed how much Andy likes cars?"

Daddy smiles proudly. "He's a real little boy."

"Andrew, look at that place. It's exquisite." Mama points to a mansion on a hill.

He knows what she's asking. He puts his arm around her. "We'll need some information before we make any decisions about living here. We need to know what makes this town tick. And what better place to find out than the local tonsilarium?"

"What about your tonsils?" Danielle says.

"Barber shop, my darling. I need a trim."

We eat ice cream cones and watch through the window while Daddy gets his hair cut. He and the barber are joking and laughing. When he's done, the barber shakes his hand and tells him to come back.

Daddy's smile slips a little as he steps out the door. "I was talking to my old friend Jim," he begins.

"Is he really your friend, Daddy?"

"Yes, he is, Polly. Mary, get a tissue. Wipe her chin. Jim says there's not much work around here. He says the place is a tourist trap and it's trapped the people who live here. Nobody can afford the rents anymore, because of all the damn bed and breakfasts. He says a bunch of people have moved over to Fort Bragg."

Mama's face crumples. "Maybe we should talk to someone else."

"He's lived here since 1953, Wendy. I believe the man knows what he's talking about."

"But can't we just try?" Mama's eyes film with tears.

"He told me about a campground down the coast a little ways. Nicer than the one we're at; it's got showers. We'll camp there until we decide what to do. Maybe we'll be able to figure out a way to stay here. Maybe. I said maybe, Wendy. Or we could check out Fort Bragg. He says there's more work there and the rents are cheaper."

"There's always more work in the cities," I say, resting Andy on my hip. Babies are heavy.

We drive south down the coast, Daddy at the wheel. His stomach hasn't bothered him all day. He's singing. We find the campground the barber described. It's right on the beach and almost empty, since most people are at work or school.

Daddy jumps out of the Wolfs' Den and lifts his arms as if he were embracing the sun. "Look at this place! Isn't it gorgeous, Wendy? Smell that air! What's it smell like to you?"

She wrinkles up her nose and sniffs. "Seaweed."

"O ye of little imagination! It smells like a new day! It smells like success!"

"It smells like seaweed to me," she says.

We set up the RV, rolling out the awning. Mama lies down for a nap with Andy and Polly.

Daddy tries to get Erica and Danielle to take a walk with us, but they snuggle on the couch and turn on the TV.

Daddy and I walk down to the water. Smooth, wet stones glisten with brilliant colors. I select the best and put them in my pocket. There aren't many shells, but there's tons of seaweed, twisted whips of it ten feet long. In the distance a man and his dog step through a veil of mist and disappear. Daddy and I are alone together, for what seems like the first time in years.

Until I was six I had my parents to myself. Having to share them with Danielle was a shock, but Daddy always made me feel special. He taught me how to fix things. He took me fishing. He talked to me like I was a person, not a kid. When he came home from work, he'd hug me and we'd play, before he even changed his clothes. One time he ran across the lawn and jumped through the sprinkler with all his clothes on; leaped right through the fan of silver water. *Andrew,* Mama shouted, *you'll ruin your new suit!* Daddy didn't care. We laughed so hard.

"This is a nice beach, Daddy."

"Yes, it's pretty." But his voice sounds distant, as if he's gone far away. Daddy, come back.

"I'm glad we're here."

"Are you really, Mary?" His eyes question mine and I know what he's asking.

"It's not so bad." I pull a rock from my pocket. It's dry now, the colors have faded. I skip it across the water. "Things could be worse."

"They have been," he says. His face looks old. Deep lines frame his sun-chapped mouth. "Mary, I'm so sorry about the way things have turned out. I didn't mean for it to be like this."

"It's not your fault."

"Oh yes it is. This whole damn thing has my name on it."

"You can't help what's happening in the country. With the economy and everything."

"It's not just that. It's a lot of things, Mary. It's— I don't know. It's kind of hard to explain. At the time, I thought I was making the right decisions. Doing what was right for my family. But now, I don't know. If I could just go back . . . But that's the thing. You can't go back. You just have to keep going, keep moving forward, even if you don't know where you're headed or what it's going to look like when you get there. . . . I did the best I could. I just want you to know that."

"I know that, Daddy."

His arms enfold me. We hold each other close. The rhythm of the waves is so peaceful.

"You're a good girl, Mary. I couldn't do it without you. And I'll make it all up to you, honey, I promise. You're going to go to school and get a college education, and have a wonderful career and a good life, Mary. You believe me, don't you?"

"Yes, Daddy."

"I'm so glad, honey. I don't want to disappoint you. I don't ever want to let you down. The world's a crazy place and it's never going to change. There's nothing you can count on but the people who love you. Your family. That's the only thing in life that really matters. You children and your mother are all I've got. I just feel so bad sometimes—"

"Don't feel bad, Daddy. Things are going to get better." Then the words spill out in a whispered rush. "We could go back to Nebraska. People would help us, Daddy. Just for a while, till we get on our feet. You'll find a job. It will all work out. We'll be happy again, you'll see."

His arms drop to his sides. The wind envelops me.

"I'll never go back. Not like this." He shakes his head. "Not after what your aunt said to me. Called me a criminal, said I was destroying my family—"

"She didn't mean it. You know she loves you. She's just worried about us, that's all."

"It's none of her business! I can take care of my family! If she likes kids so much, she should have some of her own."

"You know she can't."

"Then let her adopt some! She can't have mine! If I needed her help, which I don't, I'd ask for it. I'm sick of her sticking her nose in my business!"

"It's not just your business! It's our life, too! What about us? We're not even in school!"

"You kids are doing fine."

"You know that's not true! The girls aren't learning anything. They just watch TV. Danielle's always mad. She's just moping around. And Andy hasn't even been to a doctor yet."

"There's nothing wrong with Andy."

"Babies need to see doctors! They need checkups and shots!"

"You let me take care of that."

"You're not taking care of anything!" The look on his face warns me I should stop, but my words crash around us like waves. "You're just thinking of yourself! So you lost your stupid job! It's not the end of the world! It's just something that happened. Do we have to run away and hide forever?"

"That's enough, Mary!" he roars. "I don't have to listen to this from you."

"Then who are you going to listen to? Who'll tell you the truth? Mama? She's like a little kid! She's so scared, Daddy. She just hides in the RV and watches TV. And she steals stuff everyplace we go, taking the silverware out of that café. That makes me so ashamed. I'm so sick of this, Daddy! But nobody ever listens to me! Nobody cares about my feelings!"

Then I'm lying on the sand looking up at him suddenly, my face burning in the shape of his hand. His mouth twists, wringing words out of agony.

"Look!" he cries. "Look what you made me do! It was such a pretty day and you spoiled it, Mary. Why do you always have to spoil things? If you hate us all so much, just go back to your aunt. Just go back, if you want. I don't care what you do."

He staggers across the sand toward the RV, sobbing. It glows golden in the setting sun. I lie there for a long time, looking up at the sky, wondering who my father is becoming.

Eight

There was a mark on my cheek where Daddy's wedding ring nicked me, but Mama didn't notice and it healed quickly.

We liked that campground. The beach was safe for swimming and the bathrooms were clean. The weather was perfect and Daddy went fishing. The girls ran around like wild animals released from the cage of the RV.

I sat in the sun and read paperback books. You can get them cheap at yard sales and flea markets. I love to read. The words release me, carrying me far away. I might like to be a writer someday if anything interesting ever happens to me.

My father drove into Mendocino several times, looking for work. He came back jobless, bearing bakery goodies. The girls were happy; who cares if there's no money? We've got cookies!

"It's dead there," he said. "Business is off real

bad. Usually at this time of year they're overrun with tourists."

Mama was crushed. She'd had her heart set on one of those gingerbread houses, imagined her laundry snapping in a brisk sea breeze. Fresh sheets, sun-bleached, clean as clouds. Daddy promised her we'd live there when we made our fortune and kidded her until she smiled.

We met some people who were camping on the beach. Most of them were on vacation. So were we. Daddy told them he was an insurance man with a big office in Nebraska. Sometimes he seemed to believe it.

In the evenings I sat outside and played my guitar. One night Danielle joined me.

"What do you think's going to happen?" she said.

"What do you mean?" The chords were dull. I needed new strings.

"Do you think we're going home pretty soon?"

"I don't know," I said. "Not for a while."

"We could go back to our house. It's just sitting there empty." Danielle filled her hands with sand, then let it cover her bare feet. "What's the sense of having a house if nobody lives in it?"

"You'll have to ask Daddy about that," I said. It's not my place to tell her the truth.

"Is somebody living in it now?"

"What?"

"Do they rent it out or just let it sit there?"

"I'm not sure. I think somebody's in it."

"That's not fair. It's our house, not theirs. I want to see Grandma. I want to see Aunt Belle."

"Me, too." I hadn't talked to Aunt Belle in ages. Her calm voice always soothes me.

"Sing that song about home again."

"The Karla Bonoff song? I've played it twice already. I'll show you how to play it, if you want."

"It's too hard."

"No it's not, Danielle. You just have to try."

"Never mind. It's not important." She dusted off her feet and went into the RV.

That night I wrote a song about our family. I called it "Lost at Sea." The words were sappy but I liked the chorus.

"Where do you go when you've been everywhere

And still don't find what you're looking for there?

Where do you go when the road dead-ends

And you're standing at the edge of the sea?"

The next day a park ranger came by and told us we had to leave. You've been camped here for ten days, he said, and the rules specify a week.

No problem, Daddy says; we were planning to go; it's just such a lovely beach, etc. He tells the ranger about his company and asks him if he has enough insurance.

"When you buy insurance, you're buying peace of mind. These days, you can't have too much security." Daddy chats and jokes until they're both laughing, but his smile leaves with the ranger.

"Now what?" Mama's worried. She's been listening from the door of the RV, clasping Andy to her chest like a shield.

"What do you mean, now what? We'll go someplace else."

"Are you sure there's no work in Mendocino?"

"Of course I'm sure, Wendy. I've applied everywhere. Haven't you been listening to what I'm telling you?"

"What about Fort Bragg?" I say. "The barber said people are moving to Fort Bragg."

"Too many people. And too few jobs. The fishing and mill work have dried up," Daddy says. He runs his hand over his jaw. He could use a shave. "I think we should head south, spend a few weeks on the coast while the weather's nice, then head down the peninsula to San Francisco."

Mama hands Andy to me and crosses her arms across her chest.

"Andrew, you said no more big cities."

"We don't have to be right in San Francisco. There's a lot of towns down there. I'll find some work and a place for us to live. I want the kids to start school this fall."

"We can teach them ourselves. They're doing just fine."

Why does she say that? Mama knows it's not true. The longer we travel around like the circus, the more we seem like clowns.

"I've been giving this a lot of thought," Daddy says. "The girls need to be in school. They need to settle down. We've been fooling around long enough, Wendy."

I throw my arms around his neck.

"I can help," I say. "I'll get a job after school. I'll give you all the money for food and rent."

"You leave that to me." He strokes my hair. "You girls are going to have some catching up to do. We'll find a nice house with a good school nearby. I want to see you doing homework again, Danielle. Working on science projects. Maybe join the Girl Scouts. Make some new friends. Wouldn't you like that, honey?"

"No," she says, glaring. But she sounds so funny we all laugh.

We pack our stuff and put our trash in the Dumpster. Daddy empties out the septic tank. Then we get on Highway 1, heading south down the coast. I offer to drive but Daddy feels fine. His stomach hasn't bothered him since we've been there.

I hold Andy on my lap and sing the patty-cake song, tapping his fat fists together. He laughs.

"Look at him, Mama. Andy loves music." She smiles, but her eyes are sad. She's as shy as the girls, only used to the family, fearful of cities and strangers. "Don't worry, Mama; it's going to be fine."

She looks out the window and nods her head.

"What's that?" Daddy says.

Something's making a funny noise, and the RV's lurching to the left. Daddy pulls over to the shoulder and gets out. I hand Andy to Mama and follow him.

He looks at the engine and under the RV. Nothing looks broken or out of place. I walk back to the Jeep. One of the tires has blown out. Fat strips of rubber litter the highway.

"Well, that's just swell," Daddy says when I show him.

"Let's put on the spare."

"That's the spare," he says.

"We don't have a spare?"

"That's what I said, Mary."

"We should have a spare! We should always have a spare!"

"There's no use getting hysterical. That won't help."

"Well, now what do we do?"

"That's the question," he says. He walks back to the RV and tells Mama not to worry; it's just a tire. Then he comes back, rubbing his hands across his face.

"Can we tow it for a while?" I ask.

"Not like that. We'd be dragging it on the rim."

"We're going to have to get another tire."

"No," he says. "We're going to cut her loose."

"What do you mean?"

He looks angry, as if I'm trying to be stupid. I'm forcing him to say words he doesn't want to hear.

"We're cutting it loose, Mary. We're leaving it here. This thing is an albatross around my neck."

"We can get another tire!"

"It doesn't even run! Listen to me, Mary. Will you listen to me? We're going to have to leave it. It's too bad, I'm sorry. But we don't have the money to fix it."

"You're going to get a job. We can fix it later!"

"Mary, we're dealing with reality here. This thing has been dying since we left Nebraska. It's dead now. It's finished. That's it."

"We can't just leave it."

He gets out a wrench. He pulls off the Jeep's license plates and gets the registration out of the glove box, throwing everything into the RV's tool compartment. Then he disconnects the Jeep from the Wolfs' Den.

"Let's go," he says. "You drive."

He sits in back with his arm around Mama. When we pull away, he stares straight ahead. The little girls watch the Jeep until it disappears. No one says anything.

The campground we stay in that night is crummy. We're up early the next morning and on the road. The crack on the windshield is a river of mist. I've got the tape deck blasting and the wipers going.

Then we pass through the fog and the sun is strong.

"The banana belt," Daddy says.

"I don't see any bananas." Polly's looking around.

"What that means, honey, is that this area is sunny. Some parts of the coast have less fog than others."

"Andrew, look at those gorgeous houses," Mama says.

Enormous homes loom on either side of the road, with lots of land around them fenced by beautiful pines.

"Wouldn't you love to live here." Mama sighs.

"Most of them are probably second homes," Daddy says. Erica asks what he means, and he explains that some people have so much money that they can afford to have a house just for vacations.

"That's not fair," Erica says. "We don't even have one house."

"Yes we do, dummy. In Nebraska," Danielle says.

"Turn off here, Mary. Let's look around."

Daddy's pointing up a road. We drive into the development.

Most of the houses are two stories tall, with

walls of windows and redwood decks. A few of the houses appear occupied but most of them look vacant.

"Can you imagine having so much dough you could let one of these babies sit empty?" Daddy points out a house barely visible from the road. "Stop here, Mary."

"What're you doing, Andrew?"

"I'm going to look around for a minute."

He walks up the driveway and disappears. The empty lots on either side of the house are overgrown with brush and orange poppies.

"Look, Mama, you can see the ocean," I say.

"I know. Isn't it gorgeous? How would you like to look at that view while you're standing at the sink doing dishes?"

Daddy gets back in the RV. "Nobody home," he says. "I wanted to see if the house is available. There's usually a lot of vacation rentals in a place like this."

"Andrew, we can't afford to rent one of these houses."

"Like you always say, Wendy, you never know until you try. Mary, go back down the highway to the real-estate office. I want to get some information."

"Are we going to live here, Daddy?"

"No, we're not, you dope."

"Danielle," Mama says, "don't call your sister names."

"Are we going to live here, Daddy?" Erica doesn't give up easily.

"Probably not, honey. But we'll see," he tells her.

I drive back to the real-estate office on the highway. It's surrounded by flapping blue-and-white flags emblazoned with the name of the development: SeaScape.

Daddy puts on a fresh shirt and combs his hair. Then he goes into the office by himself. He's in there a long time.

"This is stupid," Danielle says.

When Daddy comes out of the office, he's smiling.

"Welcome to your new neighborhood," he says.

"Andrew, you're kidding. Are we really going to live here?"

"Just call me Mr. Lucky." He kisses Mama and grins. "Their maintenance-and-security man just quit. They need someone to keep an eye on the development. Do little repairs and kick out trespassers. The pay's not great, but we get a place to live for free."

Mama hugs him. "This is unbelievable!"

"I thought we were going to the city," I say.

"We are, Mary, but there's plenty of time. School doesn't start until the fall."

"Yes, but—"

"Will you quit yes-butting me and be happy for once? If I gave you the sun, you'd say, 'But

Daddy, it's hot!' I thought you'd enjoy living in one of these houses for a while."

"I would, but—"

"See, you're doing it again! I told you we'd go to the city, and we will. You and the girls will start school this fall, I promise. But it's only June. We're still on summer vacation."

He and Mama embrace. The girls jump up and down. Andy makes happy gurgly sounds.

We drive back to the secluded house Daddy inspected.

"Let's park in back," he says. "It'll be easier to unload."

The gate's jammed; he pries it open. I drive the RV into the side yard; he closes the tall wooden gate.

"I'll fix that tomorrow," he says. "Let's look at the house."

The key they gave him won't open that door, so he goes around back and lets us all inside.

Mama's in Wonderland. She's oohing and aahing. "Look at this, Andrew! Can you believe it's ours?"

We wander through a maze of spacious rooms. The furniture is new and expensive. Every room has a view of the distant, sparkling ocean. There are three bathrooms.

"Three bathrooms!" Mama says. "And a hot tub outside! I'm going to get in that hot tub and never come out."

"There's a TV!" Danielle screams. "And a

VCR!" The cabinet drawers contain hundreds of movies. She and Erica pull out their favorites, fighting over who will get the first turn.

"Look at this kitchen, Mary," Mama says. "It's got everything. A dishwasher, a microwave, a coffee maker."

"Yeah, it's got everything but food." The spotless fridge is empty except for mayonnaise and relish and butter.

"I'll go to the store as soon as we're settled," Daddy says. "There's a market a few miles down the road."

We divvy up the bedrooms. I take the one upstairs. It's private and the bed is wide and firm. Mama and Daddy will sleep in the master bedroom, with Andy and Polly just down the hall. Erica and Danielle decide to share a room. Sleeping by themselves would feel too strange and lonesome.

Mama and Daddy go to the store while Andy naps. I do laundry in the washer and dryer. It's so handy to have them right here in the house. In the TV room Erica and Danielle watch *Beauty and the Beast*. I find popcorn and a popper in a kitchen cupboard and bring them a bowl of it, slathered with butter.

Mama and Daddy return loaded down with groceries. We carry them into the house.

"Look at this stuff! We've got enough for an army!" It makes me feel rich to see all that food.

We fill up the fridge and the cupboards and bread box. Mama finds a brass bowl and piles it high with fruit, placing it on the dining room table, beneath a stained-glass lampshade.

For supper I bake chicken and potatoes and fix a big green salad. Mama and Daddy share a bottle of wine. Everybody's laughing and having a good time. Danielle helps me clean up and load the dishwasher without griping. Then she heads back to the TV room for one more movie. Andy and Polly are down for the night. Mama and Daddy sit outside in the hot tub, their soft laughter rising like steam.

I let myself out the front door and walk up the driveway. There are no streetlights, and no houses nearby. The stars glitter crisply in the sky. I can hear waves pounding on the beach across the highway. Daddy said we'll picnic there tomorrow.

Walking through the quiet night, I feel at peace. Wind whistles through the pines but it doesn't sound lonely; it sounds like the planet breathing.

I walk back to the house. It's cloaked in shadow, sheltered by the murmuring trees. An owl asks for the password. I answer: "Me." In an upstairs window a warm light glows from my room.

Nine

I get up early while everyone is sleeping and take my coffee outside on the deck. The sun presses its gleaming face to the fog. Two deer nibble the crusts of bread I threw onto the grass the night before. Mama and Daddy left the cover off the hot tub again. I replace it to keep out frogs and children.

I decide to call Aunt Belle before she leaves for work. I use the phone in the kitchen so no one will hear me.

She answers on the second ring. "Hello?" She sounds sleepy.

"Hi, Aunt Belle! It's me, Mary."

"How are you, honey? Where are you?"

"In California. Did I wake you up?"

"As a matter of fact, yes, but I'm glad you did!"

"Aren't you going to work?"

"Not today. It's Saturday."

I didn't know. We have no schedule. "I'm sorry I woke you up."

"Are you kidding? You've been on my mind so much. How are you, Mary? Are you all right?"

"I'm fine, Aunt Belle. You should see where we're living. We've got this gorgeous house right near the beach."

"Andrew's working now?" I can feel her relief.

"He's the maintenance man at this beautiful development. They give us a house to live in for free. We've even got a hot tub. There's a private beach and everything."

"Oh, Mary, I'm so pleased. You'll be staying there indefinitely?"

"Just for the summer. There's no schools around here. Daddy wants us back in school this fall."

"That's wonderful news. We've been so worried, honey. Nobody's heard from your father lately."

"Well, we've been pretty busy. We've been on the road." It's hard to speak softly; I want to shout, I'm so glad to hear her voice.

"How's the baby?"

"Fine. He's so cute. You should see him, Aunt Belle."

"I wish I could. Can you send me a picture?"

"Our camera's broken, but we're going to buy

a new one. We'll get one soon. Things are going real good."

It's true. I can see who my parents used to be, all those miles and children ago. Daddy's not so thin, and Mama's not so fat. They laugh a lot more. They're happy.

"How are the children? How's Danielle doing?" Danielle was Aunt Belle's special pet. We all were.

"She's fine. Erica, too. They love this place. They watch movies all the time. There's a VCR, and a satellite dish that gets hundreds of channels."

"And Polly?"

"She's fine. She's getting real big. She's not a baby anymore."

Aunt Belle sighed. "You give her a hug for me. She probably doesn't even know who I am."

"Yes she does. We talk about you all the time." The truth would only hurt her feelings.

"Oh, honey, I'd love to see you. Can you come back for a visit before school starts? I'll send you the money for a plane ticket."

I'm flying away, walking into the airport, searching for my aunt in a crowd of faces. "Mary!" she calls. I rush into her arms.

"Sometime, but not right now," I say. "Mama needs help with the kids. They're a handful. So how are you doing? How are Grandma and Grampa?"

"Everybody's fine, but we sure miss you guys. Does you father like his job?"

"He loves it. It's great."

"The last time we talked, you said his stomach was bothering him."

"It hasn't been, lately. He's doing fine."

"I guess he's pretty mad at me," she says.

"Not really. He knows you love him."

"Yes, I do, and I always will, even when I don't agree with him. Will you give him my love? And your mother and the girls, too? We miss you all so much. Are you playing your guitar?"

"Yeah, and I'm getting pretty good, if I say so myself. Maybe I can play for you on the phone sometime."

A door is opening, there are footsteps in the hall.

"I have to go, Aunt Belle. Andy's crying. I don't want him waking up the whole house."

"But honey, where are you? You haven't given me your phone number!"

"I'll call back soon." I hang up on my aunt. She's saying, "Mary, wait!"

Daddy's in the doorway. "Who're you talking to?"

"I was checking the time. This clock is slow." I fiddle with the dials in the coffee machine.

He stretches and yawns. "What're you doing up so early?"

"I'm not sleepy. Are you ready for some coffee, Daddy?"

"Not yet, honey. I'm going back to bed." I hear the toilet flush, then his bedroom door closing. I go out to the deck and smoke a cigarette, blowing blue fumes into the fog.

Mary, wait.

Most days Daddy's busy patrolling the development, looking for trespassers and things that need fixing. But today's his day off. He's taking the family to lunch. I offer to stay home and look after Andy. Being alone is a rare treat for me. Mama promises she'll pick up new guitar strings at the music store in Mendocino.

Andy's so alert; he notices everything. I show him the world and explain what he's seeing.

"Look at that deer, Andy. She's looking right at you. She's telling her baby: 'See that little boy?' And look, there's a squirrel way up in that tree. Can you hear the funny noise it's making?"

While Andy naps, I watch a movie, *The Godfather*. It's violent and beautiful and tragic. I study Al Pacino, watching his character change into the kind of person he always despised. The more dangerous he becomes, the more quietly he talks, his voice like a gun with a silencer.

The family returns at suppertime, bearing balloons and sunburns.

"You should've gone, Mary," Mama says. "We had a wonderful time. There was a carnival in town."

"I rode the camel!" Polly exclaims.

"You did?" I scoop her up. "What a brave girl you are."

"It had great big teeth like this! And they were all yellow!"

"See what you missed?" Daddy's face looks pink and healthy.

Erica heads for the couch. "Oooh, my tummy hurts."

"One snowcone too many," Mama says, rubbing her belly.

Danielle shoots down the hall, staking a claim on the TV.

"Did you remember my strings, Mama?"

She slaps her forehead. "Oh, Mary, I'm so sorry. I completely forgot."

Daddy put his arms around me. "We'll run up there tomorrow. Just you and me. I'll treat you to lunch."

"Don't you have to work?"

"I'll tell them it's an emergency. My best girl needs guitar strings."

Worn out from their big day, the girls go to bed early. Mama bathes Andy and puts him down. Then she and Daddy and I watch baseball.

Sometimes being the oldest feels good.

The light outside is silver and the breeze is soft, reminding me of long-ago summer nights; barbecues in our backyard with all the family, Grandma and Grampa, Aunt Belle helping Mama, a baseball game squawking on the radio, the girls chasing fireflies in the twilight.

I want to give my parents the love Aunt Belle sent them, but I know my father would refuse it.

He goes into the kitchen to make Mama some tea. He's gone a long time.

"Where did that man go?" Mama rolls her eyes. "Has he fallen asleep?"

"I'll get your tea, Mama."

"Thank you, honey. With a little milk. And see what your father is doing."

I go into the kitchen and fill her favorite mug, and set it in the microwave to boil.

There are voices outside. Daddy's talking to someone. His voice is ragged; it gets big and angry, but the man he's talking to is louder.

I move to the front door, which is slightly open. They're standing in the driveway, arguing.

The man's saying, "I don't know who you are or who the hell you think you are, but I want you out of here in five minutes."

Then Daddy's voice, all jumbled and worried, speaking so softly I can't hear him.

The man again. "Don't give me that crap. I talked to them myself, not an hour ago, and they have no idea who you are or what you're doing here. I could call the sheriff right now and have you arrested."

"No, don't do that." Daddy's pleading.

I step out the door and onto the walkway. The porch light shines on the man's face. He stands next to a van with a sign on the side that says SEASCAPE REAL ESTATE DEVELOPMENT COMPANY.

Daddy looks down, ashamed. "Mary, go back into the house."

I turn to the real-estate man.

"My name is Mary Wolf. This is my father, Andrew Wolf. He owns the largest insurance company in Nebraska. Apparently there's been some kind of misunderstanding. But you're making a greater mistake to insult him. My father's an honorable and important man."

The man and Daddy gape. I am an ape spouting Shakespeare. I am Al Pacino playing Mary Wolf.

"He's the one who's got some kind of misunderstanding," the realtor says. "You people have no business being in this house. I could call the sheriff right now and have you arrested for trespassing!"

"Call your attorney, while you're at it. I'll call the sheriff myself, if you don't stop shouting. There are children sleeping in this house and I won't have you wake them." I fire words at him, cool as steel.

"I don't know what kind of game you people are playing, but you'll have to get out of this house right now!"

"Really? The Murphys will be surprised to hear that."

That floors him. "You know the Murphys?"

"Of course," I say. "The Murphys are old friends of our family." Their name is on the beach pass on the bulletin board in the kitchen. A photograph of their children hangs over my bed. "They gave us permission to stay here. We're their guests."

"That's not what they told me on the phone just now." But the realtor's fumbling for words; he's baffled.

"I'm going to call them myself, as soon as I go inside, and tell them how badly we've been treated. They won't be pleased. Nothing you can say now will keep us from leaving. We'll be on our way tomorrow morning. However, I should point out that under California law—" Then I'm rattling off scraps from newspaper stories, civics classes, *People's Court* reruns. Mama loves to watch *People's Court*.

I drown the real-estate man in words, making him an offer he can't comprehend.

"I trust I've made myself clear," I conclude. "We'll leave tomorrow morning. In the meantime, don't bother us again."

The man is stunned. His eyeballs bulge. Has

he won or lost? He's not sure. He gets into his van and backs down the driveway, spitting up gravel in his haste to escape.

Al Pacino deserts me. I'm alone inside my head. This is no act; I am nothing but a liar. The bridge of my nose burns with tears, rage.

"Mary," Daddy whispers, "I can explain everything."

"Don't," I say, and go back into the house.

Ten

There wasn't a lot of chat the next morning. We got out of that house like refugees fleeing a hurricane, or a holocaust.

I couldn't tell if Mama knew why we were leaving. She masks her thoughts even from herself.

Danielle said, "What about your job, Daddy? Aren't you going to keep fixing things?"

"Everything's fixed," he said, stuffing groceries into a cardboard box.

"What about the trespassers? Don't they still have trespassers?"

"They're gone," Daddy said. "Get your shoes on. We're leaving."

Her angry face closed like a fist.

Daddy's stomach was killing him, so I got behind the wheel and drove down to the highway.

"Which way? Left or right?"

"Left," Daddy said. "We've already been up north."

"Where we headed?"

"South."

"I mean specifically."

"South, I said. Specifically. You heard me, Mary."

The sun was a white ball behind a sheet of fog. A few miles down the highway we stopped for milk and Rolaids at a grocery store in a tiny town called Elk.

Daddy and I got out. A hitchhiker stood near the RV; a guy maybe forty, maybe younger, if he'd had his teeth. A sack of aluminum cans was slung over one shoulder and he carried a bag of groceries with a loaf of bread sticking out.

"You know any place to camp around here?" Daddy asked him.

"Sure," the guy said. "Down the road, about fifteen miles. I'm going there now."

He wasn't going anywhere. Another car drove by.

"What's it like?" Daddy said.

"Good people. You can hang out for a while. The rangers don't hassle us much."

Daddy frowned; the man had seen through our thin disguise. We weren't a family on vacation; we were a family on the lam, looking for a hideout.

"Thanks," Daddy said. We crossed the highway and went into the store. The man was still there when we came back.

"You done with that can?" he asked me.

I finished my soda and handed him the can. He put it in his sack.

"They're worth five cents at the place in Fort Bragg. I got all these beside the highway. It's amazing what people throw out. You sure you don't want it?"

"You can have it," I said.

Daddy sat in back with Mama and Andy. I got behind the steering wheel. The hitchhiker held up his thumb, smiling.

I said to my father in the rearview mirror, "We might as well take him with us."

"Why? We don't even know him."

"He's going where we're going. He gave us directions."

"Hey, man," the guy said, "I'm not a maniac or something. What do you think: I murdered a family and stole all their groceries?" His smile was as happy and toothless as Andy's.

"You could be, for all I know," Daddy said.

"So could you, man," the guy pointed out. "I'm willing to take my chances."

He sat up front, next to me. His name was Dave.

"Thanks for the ride," he said. "My car's crapped out. It usually runs real good. It's a Mustang."

"Those are nice."

"How long you been on the road?"

"Two years or so. I don't know, exactly."

He nodded. "It's hard keeping track when you don't get the paper. I mean, how much difference is there between Saturday and Sunday?"

"Depends on the Saturday or Sunday."

"True. Mind if I smoke?'

"No."

"Yes," Daddy said.

Dave pulled out a sack of tobacco and rolled one for himself and one for me. I put on my newest Bonnie Raitt tape.

"Turn that down," Daddy said.

I turned on the fan so the smoke wouldn't bug him.

"Two years." Dave exhaled smoke. "That's a long time."

"We're on vacation," Daddy explained. "We live in Nebraska."

"Nebraska, huh? I had a girlfriend from Nebraska. Or maybe it was Kansas. Someplace back there."

"What's the campground like?" I asked him.

"The beach? It's all right. You can stay as long as you want. The rangers are pretty cool."

"Are there showers?"

"You got to be kidding. But there's outhouses and they pump them out pretty regular. It ain't bad."

"We won't be staying long," Daddy said. "I've got a job in San Francisco."

"That's great!" Dave swiveled around to look at him. "What do you do?"

"I'm in insurance."

"No kidding." Dave's face crumpled with admiration. "I had insurance on my car one time."

I followed the highway south. The fog had burned off and the sun was bright.

"Turn down here." Dave indicated a dirt road to the right.

I drove down onto the beach past a big sign alerting campers that they could stay for only one week.

"Don't worry about that," Dave said. "They don't enforce it."

"We're not going to be here long," Daddy said.

"Park over there, beside that tent," Dave said. "This rig is pretty big."

"Just for a day or two," Daddy added.

I parked the RV and we got out and looked around.

"Welcome to Lifesa Beach," Dave said. "Otherwise known as River's End."

It looked like a flea market had washed up on shore, leaving behind a wreckage of odds and ends: lawn chairs, mobile homes, kids' bikes, car parts, tires, camper shells, fishing gear, tents. Beyond the high-tide line driftwood was piled into mounds. A man crawled out of one and waved at us.

"Oh, my." Mama squinted, as if the light was too bright. She shielded her eyes with one hand and hugged Andy.

"You'll love it," Dave said. "It's like a regular little town. We've got rules and regulations, the whole caboodle. There's even a phone, up at City Hall."

"City Hall?" Daddy said.

"That phone booth by the highway." Dave's suntanned face split in a grin.

"Do we have to stay here?" Danielle wrinkled her nose. Erica huddled behind her on the RV's steps.

"Not for long," Daddy said. "There's no hookup for the RV."

"We'll have to use the generator," I said.

"I don't know," Mama murmured. "It seems kind of crowded."

Barefoot children chased each other across the sand. Dogs ran behind them, barking. Some people walked by and smiled at us. "Welcome to River's End," they said.

For several days my father was too busy to come out of the Wolfs' Den. He studied our gas receipts and maps, as if he could prove that we'd taken a wrong turn and stumbled into someone else's life by mistake.

Mama was a different story. She bloomed in the warmth of the other women, housewives and mothers like herself, good people down on their luck. These were families who'd been climbing the ladder of success; near the bottom, maybe, but nonetheless, working hard, moving up. But the rungs were rotten. Then the ladder was shattered, gone.

"We're just here till we get on our feet," they told each other. Some were working, some got county aid. River's End was a rest stop, not their final destination.

Mama began doing wash by hand at the faucet of fresh water near the highway, hanging it to dry on top of the Wolfs' Den. She'd tell the girls, "Don't go out of the yard!" Our yard extended to Bob and Vicky's blue van with the stovepipe poking through the roof, across the road to Marie and Bill's single-wide, their three kids outside fighting over one bike, and back as far as Dave and Janice's mini Winnebago, which, until we arrived, was the biggest rig. The girls weren't allowed to go down to the water by themselves or to play near the driftwood huts. Those were considered the poor side of town, occupied mostly by single men.

There were only a few people we were warned away from: a man and a woman who were always drunk and beat each other up, and a big biker named Ed with a thick gray beard who was on some kind of unpredictable drug. He spent all day working on his Harley when he wasn't kicking it apart.

Dave said there'd been a prevert at River's End, a prevert, he said, who went after the kids, but they'd run him off. Dave's wife Janice told Mama that the pervert hadn't run off; he'd disappeared. "We don't take to child molesters here," she said proudly.

The population of River's End rose and fell with the tide, people drifting in and out, but there were twenty or thirty regulars, not counting kids. There were millions of them. For once, my sisters had someone to play with besides me and each other. Danielle hung out with a girl named Marcie who lived in a big red tent, and Erica played with Marcie's brothers and sisters. Even Polly had a special friend, Megan, who lived in a blue van.

I watched them one day, moving toy cars through the sand. They didn't play house; they'd never had homes. They played Get In the Car and Drive Around. Can we stay here, Daddy? No, we're leaving. How about this place? It looks real good. Oh yes, Polly said. We'll be happy here. I love you, honey, and we won't fight.

Dave finally got Daddy to leave the RV. He came by one day and practically dragged him out. They pitched horseshoes on the beach with some other men. Daddy was a champion horseshoe pitcher back home. He returned to the RV glowing with pride and beer. He and the men sat under the awning and talked. I was sitting on the steps, reading.

The men were impressed by the grandeur of the Wolfs' Den, especially when Daddy told them how much it had cost.

"Jesus!" exclaimed the man called Abalone John. "Where'd you get that kind of dough? Steal it?"

"Insurance," Daddy said. "Headed up my own office. I had twelve guys working under me."

"Why'd you quit? Get sick of being rich?"

"Not exactly," Daddy said. "Things kind of slowed down."

"No shit." Dave shook his head and spit. "One minute we're putting up six condos a week, the next thing you know, you couldn't get a gig building a doghouse."

"Tell me about it," Louie said. "I was in real estate. People camped outside the office, wanting to buy these houses. Slept in their cars so they'd be first in line. I bought up a bunch of property myself. Then the bottom dropped out. Now I'm sleeping in my car."

"But it's a nice car," Dave said.

"And I own it, free and clear."

The men laughed. In the world they lived in before River's End, my father had been the richest, a success. True, he wasn't working now, but he had a job lined up in San Francisco. Or the prospect of a job. Or the promise of a prospect. Whatever it was, Daddy made it sound good. In the sunlight that bleached the ragged homes on the beach, the Wolfs' Den stood out like a castle.

I pass the outhouses, two wooden buildings with high, wide windows open to let in the breeze and let out the smell, and head toward the beach with my guitar. A cloud of small birds skims the waves. Kids in tattered shorts hunt shells and sand dollars. It's a pretty safe beach, no undertow, no sleeper waves to catch you off guard. I enter the path through the driftwood thicket and trip over a boy crawling out of a hut.

"Sorry. I didn't see you."

"That's okay." He stands and dusts off his knees, which poke through string where his jeans used to be.

"You live here?" I say idiotically. He's not delivering the mail.

"Yeah, it's mine. It's got my name on it. See?"

By the opening to the hut is a flat piece of driftwood with a word carved into it: Rocky.

We check each other out. He's about my age. Almost everyone else here is younger or older. Once I asked Dave where all the teenagers were. "Gone to war," he answered vaguely. Dave's a veteran, lame in one leg.

The boy's tall and skinny with pale, wild hair. The skin of his nose is roasted raw. He wears a sweatshirt with the sleeves torn off and sneakers wrapped with silver duct tape. He's holding a battered tea kettle.

"You play that thing?" He nods at my guitar.

"Sort of. Do you play?"

"No, but I like music."

"Me, too. I want to be a musician. I mean, someday, if I can."

"No kidding. That's cool."

I am badly out of practice talking to people my age. He's rusty, too. We stand there, nodding. We both start talking: No, after you.

"You been here long?" I ask.

"Maybe a week. It's okay. I been catching some fish in the river. Want some?"

"No. Not right now. I mean, thanks anyway."

"You live around here?"

"In that big thing, you can see it from here."

He looks where I'm pointing. "The RV? That's nice. It looks like it's got lots of room."

"Not for seven people."

"My place is pretty small but I like it," he says. "You want to look inside?"

"No, that's okay."

"I'll wait outside. So you won't feel funny. Don't worry, I'm not a nut or something."

Everyone here feels obliged to let you know that even though they're poor, they're not crazy.

My name is Mary Wolf and I'm not insane. I'm not a hopeless loser; I'm on vacation.

"By the way, my name is Mary."

"Rocky." We shake. "So do you want to see my place?" He's busting with shy pride.

"You sure it's okay? I don't want to butt in or anything."

"You're not. Go ahead. I'll hold your guitar."

I get down on my knees and crawl inside. The hut is maybe five feet wide and tall. A blue tarp covers the sand floor. A sleeping bag is spread beneath a hole in the wall that's curtained with a scrap of clear plastic. His knapsack, patched with duct tape, is stowed beneath a driftwood shelf that holds a few paperbacks, mostly Westerns, a candle in a saucer, a frying pan, a cracked mug, a spoon and fork, a box of wooden matches and a jar of stones and shells. Sunlight pierces the walls in a few spots where the driftwood doesn't fit snugly.

"It's nice," I say truthfully, inching back outside. "It's cozy."

"I've fixed it up a lot. It doesn't even leak. I put my name on it so nobody would steal it." He hands back my guitar and holds up the tea kettle. "I was going to get some water. Make some tea. You want some? I mean, you can if you want—you don't have to."

"Maybe in a while. I'm going down to the beach. This thing really needs new strings."

"Well, I'm going to get some water." He walks backward, looking at me. "Maybe I'll see you later."

"Okay."

"Roger," he says. "I mean, that's my real name. I like Rocky better. But you can call me what you want."

"Rocky's fine. It was nice meeting you."

He nods at me and heads toward the highway.

Eleven

When I was little, I played with neighborhood kids, but Rocky's the first real friend I've ever had. He's close to my age; he'll be eighteen in January. I feel like I've known him forever.

We hang out together. We can talk about anything. That's all we ever do, just talk. My father doesn't like him.

"You're seeing too much of that boy," he said. He had his head under the hood, changing the RV's oil. "I don't want you spending so much time with him."

"Why not?"

"Something could happen."

"Like what?"

"Like sex."

"It's not that way with us."

"I didn't say it was. But things just happen."

"Not with me and Rocky. We're friends."

"I understand that, Mary. Hand me that can of oil. He seems like a very nice boy. But he's not the kind of boy you want to get involved with."

"Why not?"

"He's a drifter."

"So am I."

"Damn it to hell." Daddy threw down the oil can so hard it bounced. Mama stuck her head out of the RV, saw our faces, and withdrew. "That's not true. Why do you say things like that? You know I've got a job lined up in San Francisco. We'll be moving soon."

"A real job? Since when?"

"Are you calling me a liar?"

"It seems like you didn't have a job, now you do."

"The point is this, I'm not having you involved with somebody like that, some kid you don't even know his background."

"He knows my background and he still likes me. At least he's not prejudiced like you!"

"Do you hear what I'm saying?"

"You can't tell me what to do!"

"Come back here when I'm talking to you!"

I kept walking. He's worried about money lately and takes it out on me. Mama hasn't been doing her flea market gig; the last time scared her, and anyway, there's nothing around here worth stealing. Daddy's made a couple of phone calls from City Hall, trying to borrow money from my grandparents. Grampa said no and Daddy got real mad. Then he got ahold of Grandma and she promised to send some to the Western Union office in Fort Bragg. Dave's taking him up there this week. Daddy doesn't drive the RV unless he has to; it uses too much gas. Dave's real nice, he gives people rides. A lot of people here don't have cars that run.

His wife Janice takes Mama to the free-food pantry in Fort Bragg. Andy usually stays with me. He's bigger every day, roly-poly and pink. The disposable diapers got too expensive, so we're using cloth ones, which we wash by hand. They dry stiff in the wind and chafe his skin.

I wish she'd take him for his vaccination shots. Polly had them so she wouldn't get a disease. Some of the women here think the shots are unnecessary. They say they might even make your baby sick. Mama never used to believe that, but she bends in the breeze of the strongest opinion.

She's been trying to talk Daddy into applying for welfare. Some of the families get county aid and are telling Mama we might qualify, too. It's a complicated process but it's worth a shot. Daddy flatly refuses.

"What's your self-respect worth, Wendy?" he brayed the other night. The volume goes up when he's been drinking beer. "Are you willing to trade your pride for food stamps?"

I was sitting at the table, making the girls

practice their handwriting. Mama cringed and didn't answer him. That made me angry.

I said, "I guess I'll fix a side of pride for supper tonight. Daddy, how do you want yours cooked?"

"You shut your mouth."

"Don't talk to me like that. You always act like this when you've been drinking."

"I haven't been drinking! Just a few beers."

"Pardon me if I don't get the distinction."

"You mind your own business."

"It is my business. You're scaring the girls."

"I'm not scared," Danielle sneered, throwing down her pencil.

"They're not scared," Daddy said. "Come here, Polly. You're not scared of me, are you?"

He got her giggling. Erica butted her head against him until he tickled her, too.

"Daddy, do you mind? We're doing some studying so the girls won't be so behind in school."

"For God's sake, Mary, will you relax? You sound like an old lady. There's plenty of time for the girls to catch up. We're still on summer vacation."

Erica's head was on his knee. She turned toward me and stuck out her tongue.

"I'll tell you one thing," I tell Rocky, "I'm not having any kids."

We're leaning against a log on the beach, watching the thick green waves roll in.

"Ever?"

"Maybe."

"Don't you like your sisters?"

"Yeah, but once you have kids, you're not free anymore."

"Your parents are free. They go where they want."

"No they don't. They just go."

I'm plunking out chords; Mama bought me new strings. Rocky's cutting up an apple with his pocketknife. He pops a slice into my mouth.

He says, "I'd like to see my brother. I hope he's doing okay."

"You could call him."

"No money."

"You could call collect."

"They don't like that," he says, meaning the foster parents who took them in when their mother left. One day when he and Bobby came home from school, her clothes were gone. She'd left the rest; there wasn't much to take. It was a shock, Rocky said, but no surprise. He fixed supper for Bobby and they went to bed. They thought she might come back. She had before.

This time she didn't, and she didn't call. After a while, the school found out. They had an uncle in town but he didn't want them, so the county placed them in a foster home. At least they got to stay together. When he was fourteen, Rocky walked away. He didn't need to run, he said; no one was coming after him.

"Why'd you leave?"

"I don't know." He hands me another slice of apple. "It wasn't like they whipped us or anything. It was just kind of nothing. Their duty, you know, and the county gave them money for having us. At Christmas they'd give us these teeny little toys; then we'd sit there and watch their real kids open all these presents. Bikes and things. They always bought us used clothes. The bigger I got, the less I fit in there. Soon as I can, I'll have Bobby with me."

"Does he like it there?"

"He says he does. The last time I called he only talked a minute; then he wanted to watch TV."

"Kids are weird." I light a cigarette.

"Why do you do that?"

"Smoke, you mean? Because I'm a stupid idiot."

"No, really."

"Really. That's the reason." I exhale poison, enveloping Rocky and me. I stink.

"So why do you do it?"

"I'm nervous, I guess. Anyway, it gives me something to do with my hands besides strangle my father."

"He seems real nice."

"He used to be."

"People change," Rocky agrees.

"Especially him."

"My mother changed, but not a lot. She always said she didn't like kids. I don't know why she had us."

"Just did, probably."

"But after she had me, she must've known she didn't want any more, so why'd she have Bobby?"

"Adults do lots of stupid things. Where's your father?"

"Los Angeles, I think. He left before Bobby was born. He and my mother had terrible fights."

"They must've liked each other sometimes. For at least five minutes."

"Who knows?" Rocky sighs. "They're gone now."

The apple feels gritty between my teeth. The wind's always blowing, seasoning everything with salt, tangling my hair like seaweed. When I clean the girls' ears, they're full of sand.

"If you were stranded on a desert island and could only have one thing with you, what would it be?" I ask.

"A telephone, so I could send out for pizza."

"No, really."

"Just one thing? Besides you, you mean? Duct tape, I guess."

"You and your duct tape."

"It's mighty handy stuff. What would you take?"

"My guitar, I guess. Or a never-ending book. I'm running out of things to read." I've been borrowing paperbacks from Mama's friends, but most of them are romance or horror.

"Yeah, it'd be nice to have a library around here."

"It'd be nice to have anything around here," I say. "Let's face it: This *is* a desert island."

"It's not that bad. We're not trapped here forever."

I'm not so sure. Daddy's settling in, talking less often about San Francisco. People look up to him; they ask his opinion. He's admired by everyone but a former car salesman who was the resident bigwig until my father arrived. Daddy's organized a softball team and a police force. He and Dave practice target shooting near the cliffs. Dave traded him a gun for a Confederate flag Mama picked up in a flea market.

Some of the people have lived here for years. They say the beach is brutal in the winter, bleak and freezing. Summer's the easy season. There's plenty of fish and wild blackberries, and vegetables grown in inner-tube gardens. Once a week people drive up to the food pantry in Fort Bragg and get day-old bread and canned goods and powdered milk. We have potluck cookouts. Everybody shares. If we ever get to leave, I'll miss these people.

"When do you think you'll be moving?" Rocky asks casually, as if he's checking the time. It's a painful subject. I want to leave River's End, but I don't want to say good-bye to him.

"Pretty soon. We've got to find a place to live before school starts. Do you think you'll be heading down that way?"

"Maybe. I've got to find some work."

"What about school?"

He shrugs. "Maybe later. The main thing now is making some money. I might go inland, over near Cloverdale. Dave says there's some fairs there in the summer."

"Be a carny person? Your teeth are too good. Carny people have terrible teeth."

"Dentists cost money," Rocky says quietly.

We haven't been to a dentist in years. Erica's teeth poke out like a beaver's. I try to get her to quit sucking her thumb. I will, she promises, but it slides back in. She doesn't even know she's doing it.

I stand and brush sand off my jeans. "I better get back and help Mama with supper. You want to eat with us?"

"You should check with them first."

"Good idea. Can I use your phone?"

"I mean, maybe they don't want me coming over all the time."

"You don't come over all the time. It's fine."

"I can bring some bread."

"Save it for later. We've got plenty of food." Daddy won't be pleased to see him, but that's not news.

As we climb the beach, jagged words blow in our faces. A man named Joe is yelling at his son. Janice says Joe beats up his wife. The wife tells people, "I'm so dorky. I fell down," a shamefaced grin beneath her blackened eyes.

Now her little boy falls down while she wrings her hands and pleads, "Joey, don't. Joey, please, he didn't mean to!"

Joe slaps the kid's face and punches his arm. Smacks his head. The little boy's crying.

Something sharp tears loose inside me. I'm sick of hearing children cry.

"Leave him alone!" I say. "You can't hit him like that!"

"I can't?" Joe looks at me, amazed, almost smiling.

"Are you crazy? He's just a little boy! Why don't you pick on somebody your own size?"

The man's eyes measure me. "How about you?"

"You could try," I say. "I wouldn't advise it."

Rocky steps between us. "Come on, Mary. We'll go get your dad."

"Back off. I can handle this." I push him aside. Fury has burned up all my fear.

Joe snarls, "Didn't anybody ever teach you to mind your own business?"

"It is my business. You can't hit him like that."

"He's my kid! I can do what I want!" Joe steps toward me. "I can hit anybody I feel like!"

"Try it. Go ahead. See what happens." My tingling fingers curl into fists.

"You're crazy." Joe sneers, but he looks uneasy.

"That's right, I am." I feel hard as stone. I could pound him to death with my heart.

"Mary, let's go get your dad," Rocky begs.

"He's not your property! You can't treat him like that! If you and your wife want to kill each other, go ahead! Everybody here will be glad. But leave him out of it! He's just a little kid! You're supposed to love him, not hurt him!"

I'm yelling so loud that people come running; Dave and Janice and some others. My father shoulders through the crowd, inflated with self-importance and worry.

He's stunned to see me. "Mary, what are you doing?"

"Telling this jerk he can't beat up his kid."

"This bitch—" Joe begins but Daddy's got him by the throat, bent across the hood of his old wrecked car.

"Wait a minute! Wait a minute!" Dave pulls them apart. "Let's everybody calm down. Joey, come on, man!"

"It's none of her business what I do!"

"Come on, man," Dave says. "We're all good people here. She's just trying to help."

"She can help by butting out! Ask my wife; the kid got what he deserved! Ask my wife! She'll tell you!"

The woman doesn't speak up, for her husband or her son. She leans against Janice, sobbing. The little boy scowls at everyone, as if we're the biggest crowd of clowns he's ever seen.

Daddy turns on Rocky. "What're you standing there for? Why didn't you defend her?"

"I don't need defending! You know what I need?" I shout at my father, at the circle of faces. "I need people to act like grown-ups for a change! There's rules, you know! Rules and regulations!"

"Mary's right," Dave says. "Joe knows better than that. He just got a little carried away."

"That's bullshit," I say. "The guy's a psycho. And she's just as bad. What're you crying for, lady? For yourself or your little boy? You and this bozo can beat each other to a pulp. I don't care what you do. You can hit the road. But the boy stays here, with people who'll love him."

"He's not your kid!" she wails. "You can't take him!"

"No, but the county can. All I have to do is make one phone call—"

"That's enough, Mary," Daddy says. "You're not in charge here."

"Then who the hell is?"

"Calm down, Mary. We'll take care of it," Dave promises. "Joe knows he can't act that way."

"You're listening to her? I don't believe this!" But beneath his bluster, Joe's scared. His car doesn't run. He depends on Dave.

"Remember what I said. I'll be watching you," I warn him.

"Mary, did you hear me?" Daddy says. "Go home."

"I don't have one." I stare into my father's eyes until he turns away.

Twelve

"Mary," Daddy said, "what you need to understand is that we're living on the new frontier."

He aimed the pistol and fired. A hole bloomed in the target. He handed me the gun. "You try it."

"I hate guns, Daddy."

"I hate them, too. But the world's full of nuts."

"And I don't want to be one."

"Go ahead and shoot."

"Why do I have to do this? Why can't Mama learn instead of me?"

"You know she won't. It's too much for her, Mary. Aim at the circle in the middle. That's his heart."

"We never had any guns before. Why do we have to have one now?"

"Look around you, honey," he said gently.

"I'm not just talking about this place. The whole country's changed. Life's different now. People used to care, used to help each other out. Now some of them would kill you for a parking space."

"Great," I said. "This will sure come in handy at the supermarket."

We were way down the beach, where the sand ends in cliffs. The blue-gray pistol was heavy and small. I raised the gun and fired. A hole appeared in the plywood, almost at the instant I heard the shot.

"This thing's too loud."

"A little noise won't hurt you. Try again."

"Daddy, what's the point? I could never use a gun on a real person."

"Not even if that person was hurting your family? What if a stranger threatened Mama and the kids? Would you stand there and say, 'Please don't hurt us, Mr. Nutcase!'?"

"Maybe, unless he was made of wood. Anyway, you'd get him."

"I might not be home. I might be at work. You're the oldest, Mary. These are things you need to know."

"Not in San Francisco."

"The city's even worse. No place is really safe these days. You know that. You read the newspapers."

"Then Mama should learn, too."

He looked patient and pained. "Mama's a girl."

"What's that make me?"

"Don't make that face. You know what I mean. I can't even get her to drive a car. Mama grew up in a different time. She was raised for a world that doesn't exist anymore."

"It never existed."

"You're too hard on your mother. She's not strong like you. She needs people to love and protect her."

"She's not a child."

"I didn't say she was. Here, let me show you how to load it."

"What did Mama do before she met you?"

"Waited for me to come and rescue her." He smiled. "Worked in her parents' store. Your mama's not one of these modern gals who wants to make a lot of noise and rule the world. All she ever wanted was a home and family."

"Well, she got the family."

He shot me a look. "No way I'll get a swelled head with you around. Isn't it sad that I command more respect from the people at this campground than I do from my own daughter?"

"Very," I said, but he missed the point. He thought I was apologizing.

"Sad, but that's the way of the world. A prophet is never recognized in his own country."

He handed me the pistol. I pushed the hair out of my eyes. The wind was blowing strong.

"Daddy," I said, "don't take this wrong, but

you're not a prophet; you're an insurance salesman. The people here look up to you because you used to be rich, compared to them. You're sitting there in that big RV. They're living in cars and tents. And you always sound like you know what you're talking about."

"Even when I don't, you mean."

"Yes."

He looked shocked; then he laughed. He put his arm around me. "Honey, I can count on you to keep me honest. Let's face it: I'm selling hope to the hopeless, the insurance for people who've got nothing left to lose. Hold it steady and aim for the center."

"I don't want to do this! We're wasting bullets."

"Look around you, Mary. It's a crazy old world. We didn't make it that way and we sure can't change it. All we're trying to do is survive. Take a shot."

I steadied the gun and pulled the trigger. The bullet pierced the middle of the target.

"Not bad!" Daddy said. "You're learning."

Dave came loping down the beach, his bad leg swinging.

"Andrew, you better come up," he called.

"What's the matter? Trouble?"

"The rangers are here. Freddy's been mooning the people on the ridge again."

"That was smart." Daddy grimaced. "What an idiot."

"Well, I know," Dave said. "But once he starts drinking, he stops thinking."

High above River's End is a ridge fronted with huge new homes. The people who live up there don't like us. We ruin their expensive view. This isn't the first time they've complained to the rangers, but so far nothing bad has happened.

"We better see what they want." Daddy pockets the pistol and we hurry up the beach to the campground.

The rangers are waiting beside our RV, sunglasses masking their tanned faces. Mama stands by the back end, holding Andy, picking at the flag decal on the window, rolling pieces into tiny balls. A small crowd has gathered, talking and laughing, waiting to see what's going to happen.

"Rita! Tom!" Daddy greets them warmly. He has a talent for remembering names. He says that comes in handy in business. "Can I get you some iced tea? Wendy, get some glasses."

"No, thanks, Andrew. We just wanted to let you know that we've had some complaints." Tom nods toward the ridge. "Somebody's been mooning them."

"Hmmm," Daddy says. "Sounds mighty serious. Good thing they have binoculars or they couldn't tell."

The people on the ridge aim telescopes at us, as if they were studying an enemy encampment.

Tom grins. "Well, I know. Personally, I don't

care. But you guys aren't even supposed to be here. Things like this don't help."

"We'll take care of it," Daddy promises. "We don't want any trouble."

"They say your dogs chase their cats. They've heard gun shots," Rita adds.

Daddy shakes his head, puzzled. "You can't shoot a gun on the beach. We know that."

"They want the beach cleared. They say it's a public nuisance."

"They're the nuisance!" Dave exclaims. The crowd mutters agreement.

Tom holds up his hands to quiet them. "We're not saying they're right and we're not saying they're wrong. But if word comes down, we'll have to enforce it."

"You can't!" Dave cries. "We've been living here for years. Where would all these people go?"

"Just calm down, Dave," Daddy says. "Rita and Tom are trying to help."

"We've looked the other way for a long time," Tom reminds us.

"We know that." Daddy nods. "You've been awfully kind. You'll let us know if anything changes?"

"You'll know as soon as we do," Rita promises.

"They'll never get us out of here," Janice tells the crowd. "This is our beach, too! Those people up there don't own it."

"Well, I know that," Tom says, "but they think they do. And the state's starting to talk about clearing the beach. It might be a good idea for you people to look for another place, just in case."

"Like where?" someone shouts. "Up on the ridge? Look around you, man. People are hurting!"

"We know that," Rita says. "But the state makes the rules, not us."

"What is this, Russia? What's happened to people's rights?" someone shouts. The crowd's turning ugly.

"We didn't come here to argue. We're just doing our job."

"We appreciate that, Rita, we really do. But people can't just pick up and leave," Daddy says. "They've lived here for years. They have nowhere to go."

"We're not saying you have to leave right now. But those people up there are making lots of phone calls. It's better to plan ahead."

"Tom, Rita, we want to thank you for coming down here. And we'll take care of those little problems you mentioned." Daddy shakes their hands. "Can you join us for dinner? We're having a cookout."

"Barbecued rich people," someone says. People laugh.

"Thanks anyway," Tom says. "We'll be on our way."

They get into their truck and drive off. Daddy says, "Where's Freddy?"

"In his tent," Janice says.

"Get him up here. Get everybody up here. We've got to have a meeting."

Mama touches his arm, scared. "Andrew, what's happening? Does everybody have to leave?"

"Not if I can help it." He looks exhausted.

"What should I do? Should I make some coffee?"

"For God's sake, Wendy, we're not having a party. The world's ending and you're serving refreshments."

"Don't get mad at her. It's not her fault."

"It's all right, Mary."

"No it's not, Mama. He doesn't need to talk to you that way."

Daddy glares at me, then glances at Mama. Her chin is quivering. He draws her close. "I'm sorry, honey. I didn't mean to snap at you. I'm just so tired."

"It's all right, darling." Mama hands Andy to me and rubs Daddy's shoulders.

Within minutes most of the people at the campground are milling around outside the Wolfs' Den, even the men from the driftwood huts.

"What's up?" Rocky asks me, tickling Andy's toes.

I nod toward the ridge. "They want us out of here."

"They don't own the beach. They can't make us leave. Can they?"

I shrug. My father's talking.

"We just had a visit from the rangers," he tells the crowd. "Seems someone has offended our upstairs neighbors."

"Poor things!" someone shouts. "We've hurt their feelings."

"They don't have any feelings," someone says.

"This is serious." Daddy frowns. "They could get us kicked out. We're not supposed to be living here in the first place."

"We're not hurting anybody! We're not ruining the beach!"

"I know that," Daddy says calmly, as if he's talking to children. "But the rules specify a one-week stay. We're way over the limit. The last thing we want to do is give them an excuse to boot us out."

"We've changed the rules! This is our beach now! We were here before they built those houses up there."

"I realize that, John, but who's the sheriff going to listen to, them or us? Now if Freddy could keep on his damn pants—"

"So I mooned them!" Freddy shouts. "Big deal! So what!" He's a skinny man, swaying in the breeze of too much beer. "They couldn't even tell if they didn't use their goddamn spyglasses!"

"But they do use them, Freddy! They do! That's the point! Exposing yourself is a public offense."

"I was just being friendly."

"Then smile and wave! When you see those glasses on you, do this! Hello! Hello up there!" Daddy grins and waves hugely. Laughter ripples through the crowd. "We don't need to sink to their level, people. We're better than them. We stay nice and polite."

"That won't work," Dave says grimly. "We could go around in tuxedos and they still wouldn't like us. They're going to try to kick us out."

"Maybe," Daddy says. "But there are things we can do. We're not helpless. We can make phone calls, too. We can talk to the newspapers and the TV people. How would that look on the evening news; all you nice people getting kicked off the beach? We can drive up to the county and visit our supervisors. How would they like to see us walk in, with our wives and our kids and our babies? We've got a lot going for us, people, but we've got to stick together and use our heads. No mooning the neighbors, no dogs chasing their cats—"

"Dogs chase cats," Freddy says. "That's what they do."

"Who's in charge, Fred; you or your dog? We

tie up the dogs. We don't give these people any ammunition. If we do, it'll be our own damn fault. Do you understand what I'm saying?"

"Anyway," Freddy says, "who elected you God?"

Everybody looks at Daddy, waiting.

"The twelve disciples," he snaps. "You've got a better idea? Come on, Fred, we're all waiting to hear it."

Freddy hangs his head. "I didn't mean nothing. It's just, you know, it's a bunch of bull."

"I agree with you, my man, but we play by the rules or we're going to get thrown out of the game."

"Andrew, can they really make us leave?" someone asks.

"I don't know, Ruth. But even if they can, nothing's going to happen right away. These things take time. We can talk to a lawyer."

"Not without money," Dave says mournfully. I've never seen him so discouraged.

"O ye of little faith! What's the matter with you, Dave? Haven't you heard of public-interest lawyers? We're the people, remember? And this is still America. In the meantime let's all keep our cool. We're going to make those people on the ridge love us. They'll love us so much they'll want to adopt us."

Dave points to the ridge. "They're watching us right now." Sunlight glints off their binoculars.

"You know what to do, people."

The crowd follows Daddy's lead. They turn toward the ridge, smiling and waving. A few tip their hats and tap-dance.

Laughing, they drift off to fix their suppers. Some shake Daddy's hand and thank him.

"Andrew, man, I don't know what we'd do without you," Dave says, his voice breaking.

"Don't worry," Daddy tells him. "Everything's going to be fine."

I ask Daddy if Rocky can join us for supper.

"Not tonight," he says. "It's a family time."

"He won't eat much."

"Not now, I said."

The show's over. I tell Rocky I'll see him tomorrow.

In the Wolfs' Den, Mama's warming soup. Danielle wants to go to the cookout.

"Not tonight," Daddy says. "We've got to make some plans."

"What kind of plans?" Mama asks.

"We're leaving."

"Now? But you said—"

"I know what I said. But any fool can see the writing on the wall. It's just a matter of time before they close the beach and kick us out."

"But I thought—"

"Don't think, Wendy. Let's just eat."

She passes around bowls of tomato soup and a plate of cheese sandwiches.

"If you think we've got to leave, you should've told them the truth," I say.

"Right." Daddy grunts. "That would've gone over good."

"But what about the lawyer and the TV people?"

"Listen to me, Mary. I'm not Jesus Christ. I'm just an unemployed salesman, as you so often point out. These people don't want help; they want a baby-sitter. They want someone to solve all their problems. I've got enough problems of my own."

"But Marie's got a skirt on her trailer," Mama says.

"Then they'll have to take off the skirt or dump the trailer. I don't know what they're going to do. All I know is, we're hitting the road before the rangers come back with an eviction notice."

"I don't want to leave!" Erica wails.

"Don't you want to go to school? Don't you want to live in a nice house?"

"No! I want to stay with my friends!"

"You'll make new friends," he says.

"I don't want to make new friends!"

Danielle says, "Don't we even get a vote?"

"No."

"I thought this was America."

"Just eat your dinner."

"I don't want to eat! I'm not hungry!" she shouts.

So fast we don't even see it coming, Daddy grabs her bowl and hurls it into the sink. It shatters. Soup splatters across the counter.

Now Danielle's crying and Erica starts. Andy studies them, his eyes alarmed. I pick him up and cuddle him close.

"Look, Daddy, I'm eating." Polly slurps her soup.

"So when are we leaving?" I don't feel glad. I can picture Rocky's face when I tell him we're going.

"Soon as we can. I'll check out the RV tomorrow. The battery might need recharging."

"What are you going to tell Dave?"

"What do you mean, what am I going to tell him? I'm going to tell him we're going. He's a grown man. He can take care of himself. For Christ's sake, Mary, we hardly even know him."

"He thinks you're his friend."

"I am his friend. But it's every man for himself. Dave knows that."

"I'm sure glad I'm not a man," I say. I wrap Andy in his blanket and carry him outside and down the beach toward Rocky's hut.

Thirteen

Rocky's hut glows in the dusk like a jack-o'-lantern. I knock at the entrance.

"Avon calling."

"Come on in." He's glad to see us. He takes the baby. I crawl inside.

"I hope we're not interrupting your supper."

"I'm done."

"What'd you have?"

"Bread." He looks embarrassed. "You want some?"

"No, thanks. I'm fed up with my father."

"What's wrong?"

"Oh, nothing," I say. "Just everything."

I set Andy on the tarp and Rocky gives him the roll of duct tape. Andy tries to cram it in his mouth.

"He'll make it all wet."

"That's okay, he can't hurt it."

"You'd be amazed. I think he's teething. Do you have something else he can chew on?"

Rocky lights another candle and looks around. He gives Andy a balled-up sock. "Don't worry. It's clean. And I've got something for you." He hands me a flattened, unsmoked Kent. "I found it on the beach today."

"Thanks, but I don't smoke around the baby. I'll save it for later."

"You shouldn't smoke around yourself."

"Then why are you giving me a cigarette?"

"I don't know." He looks guilty. "I thought you might like it."

"I'm sorry. I'm acting like a jerk," I say. "Things are a little tense on the homefront."

"Your father made a really good speech tonight."

"That's all it was. Just a bunch of words." Andy's propped against my legs, sucking on the sock. "He didn't mean a thing he said. We've leaving as soon as the RV's ready. Maybe tomorrow."

"Why?" Rocky's shocked. "He said we could stay here."

"He says it's just a matter of time before the rangers kick us out. He's probably right."

"Then why didn't he tell us?"

"Nobody wanted to hear that. He's a salesman, you know; he wants people to like him."

"They do."

"I don't."

"Mary, you don't mean that." The candle-light flickers; shadows lap his face. "He's a pretty good guy. At least you have a dad. I don't even know where mine's at."

"I don't know where mine's at, either. Sit up, Andy. You're falling over. See how he can hold up his head by himself now?"

"He's strong," Rocky says proudly. "Look at this grip." Andy grabs Rocky's finger. "Let go, let go!" Andy laughs, a little snicker. "He's sure a good baby."

"He really is. And they're not even taking him for his vaccination shots."

"Why not?"

"Mama's too lazy."

"No she's not."

"She sits around on her butt all day and talks to her friends, that's all she does. You just think any mother is better than yours."

Rocky's face gets stiff. "Well, she hasn't taken off."

"I wish she would. I wish they'd both disappear. They act like a couple of idiots. I'm the only one who really cares about the kids and everybody hates me."

Tears slide down my cheeks. I'm surprised to be crying. Rocky hands me a T-shirt to dry my face.

"Don't worry, it's clean," he says.

"Well, I'm not. I'd give a hundred bucks to take a shower. I'm so sick of this place."

The tears won't stop. I hide my face. Rocky reaches over and pats my shoulder.

"The trouble is, where are we supposed to go? We don't have any plans, we don't have any money."

"What about your dad's job in San Francisco?"

I answer him with a look.

"What about your aunt? She'd send you some money."

"My dad would rather die than take it. You should hear him talk. He blames her for everything. You'd think it was her fault he lost his job. Anyway, so what if he lost his job? Lots of people do; it's not the end of the world, unless you make it that way."

"People are different."

"Well, he's sure different. I feel like I don't even know him anymore."

Andy's face lights up with a brilliant grin. "Bub bub bub," he says.

"Bub bub bub to you, too." I hug him. "I'm sorry, I didn't mean to come here and fall apart. I just had to get out of that place for a while."

"I'm glad you did. I could make you some tea."

"That's okay, we have to get going soon. This guy will want to nurse before he goes to sleep."

"You could come with me, if you want to," Rocky says softly, glancing at my face, then down at his shoes.

"Come with you where?"

"When I leave, I mean." Now he's looking out the doorway at the violet sky, sprinkled with a few bold stars.

"You mean work at a carnival?"

"Until we find something better. It sounds kind of stupid. It was just an idea."

"I can't leave my family. They'd fall apart. Or maybe they wouldn't, I don't know what they'd do. All I know is, it wouldn't be good."

"I know," he says. "I'm not saying you should go. I'm just saying you can if you want to."

"Thanks."

We sit in the doorway, watching the night seal the sky and the water together. It's cold; the breeze is laced with fog. Rocky drapes his sleeping bag across our shoulders. Andy's snug in my lap, chewing on my braid. For a long while we're silent, listening to the waves.

"It's nice here," he says. "Too bad we can't stay."

"I want to go to school."

"You're smart. You'll do good."

"You're smart, too."

"Not like you," he says.

"Yes you are. You could do anything you want, but you have to get an education."

"That costs money."

"High school's free."

"Nothing else is, rent or food. Mary, can I ask you something?"

"Sure."

"Wait a minute." He gets up and gets his toothbrush and water jug and steps outside and brushes his teeth. Then he sits beside me again. "Mary, would it be okay if I kissed you?"

"That would be okay."

"You don't have to if you don't want to."

"I know."

"Are you sure?"

"I'm sure."

His face comes close. His lips are soft. His breath smells sweet as Andy's.

"Thanks," he says. That makes us laugh.

"I've never kissed a boy before."

"Me neither." We laugh some more then kiss, gently.

"That's nice. I really like you, Rocky."

"I like you, too, Mary. A lot." We hold hands.

"I don't want to leave you, but I don't want to stay here."

"I know." He sighs. "I don't want you to go. I wish things could turn out different."

Andy wriggles and twists his head toward my chest.

"Sorry, bud, I don't have the equipment. I better get him back to Mama."

Rocky helps us outside. "I'll walk you home."

"Better not, my dad would have a fit. He wasn't in a real good mood when I left."

"Take my flashlight. The batteries are new. Dave gave me some money for collecting cans."

"Thanks. Thanks for everything."

"No problem. Anytime. The door's always open."

"You don't have a door."

"No wonder it's always open." We smile. "Will I see you before you go?"

"Oh, sure. It takes a while to get all packed up. It's kind of like getting the circus on the road. I'll bring your flashlight back tomorrow."

"Okay. Well, good night."

"Good night."

I step forward and kiss him, then trace the shape of Rocky's face, his lips, as if I could store the feel of him, imprinted on my fingertips.

"Now I'm really going." Lugging Andy on my hip, I follow Rocky's flashlight through the darkness.

Fourteen

We couldn't leave the next day because the RV wouldn't start. The battery was dead.

"Goddamn sonuvabitch." Daddy pounded the hood.

I was sitting there, watching. "That won't do any good."

He looked like he wanted to pound me, too.

He called around from the phone at City Hall. Nobody had the right-size battery in stock. A parts store in Fort Bragg said they could have one in a week.

Daddy warned us not to tell anyone we planned to leave.

"Why not?" Erica asked. We were eating lunch. Mama was feeding Andy mashed banana.

"It's none of their business what we do or don't do. They'd get all worked up, maybe want to come. I'm not taking anybody with me."

"Not even me, Daddy?"

"Of course I'm taking you, Polly. Just be quiet and eat your lunch."

"Have you called the people in San Francisco about your job?" I asked. "You know, to make sure it's still available?"

"You leave that to me. I'll find a job."

"I thought you had a job. That's what you said."

"You mind your own business."

"It is my business! It's my life, too! You're not the king."

He slammed down his cup. Coffee sloshed onto the table. Mama mopped it up with the hem of her skirt.

"And you're not the queen! I'm sick of your attitude! Since when are you in charge?" he shouted.

"You don't even know where we're going to go! We can't go anywhere; this thing is dead."

"It's just the battery. We'll be leaving next week."

"Leaving for where? What'll we do when we get there?"

"I told you! I'm getting a job in San Francisco and you girls are going to school!"

"I don't want to go to school. I hate it," Erica pouted.

"Just hush," Mama whispered, "and finish your lunch."

"I don't want to go to San Francisco," Danielle said. "I want to see Grandma. I want to see Aunt Belle."

"Shut up, Danielle. Not one more word."

"Andrew, please." Mama tried to touch his arm.

"Don't you 'Andrew, please' me! What's the matter with you people?" He stood, knocking over his chair. "Isn't anybody listening to me? We'll go where I say when I say we're going! End of discussion! I blame you, Mary. You're poisoning this family. You're turning these girls against me!"

"I just asked you a question: Where the hell are we going?"

"Mary," Mama murmured, "there's no need to swear."

"Mama, can we please get serious here for one minute? How long can you pretend that everything's fine? We don't have any money, we don't have any plans—"

"We're going to San Francisco! You heard me, Mary."

"Let's go home," Danielle said. "Let's go back to our house. We can make the people leave and we can live there."

"We can't," Daddy said. "It's out of the question."

"Why not?"

"Because we can't."

"Why not, Daddy?"

"Because I said so!" he roared in her frightened face. She tried not to blink, but tears spilled down her cheeks, scorching me, igniting my rage.

"Why don't you tell her the truth?" I said. Mama's eyes pleaded with me, but I couldn't stop. "Just tell her the truth. Or don't you know it anymore?"

"You shut your mouth. I'm warning you, Mary!"

"We don't have a house, Danielle. Daddy sold it. We don't have a house to go to."

"You're lying!" she shouted. "We do so have a house!"

"He sold it and he didn't even tell Mama. He forged her name on the papers."

Daddy lunged across the table and grabbed my neck. "Goddamn you, shut up! Shut up or I'll kill you!"

I seized his wrists. He was squeezing my throat. All I could see were his eyes.

"Andrew, stop! You're hurting her! Andrew!"

Mama's voice reached him. He shuddered and released me. I sagged to my knees, gasping for breath.

"Get out of here," he said, turning his back. "Just get out."

"It's not true, is it, Daddy?" Danielle said as I left. "It's not true what Mary was saying."

I'm running toward the highway. I'll hitch a ride, back to Nebraska, to Aunt Belle's house. Oh, Aunt Belle, things have gotten so bad. They've gotten so bad and I don't know how to fix them. I'm too old to play the game of Let's Pretend anymore. But everybody hates me when I tell the truth.

Aunt Belle, I never meant to lie to you.

I stand beside the highway and stick out my thumb. A few cars pass but nobody stops. Who stops for a crying girl? She might be crazy. The world's full of nuts. Don't ride with strangers. My father's a stranger and Mama's a child, slipping backward in time, younger every day. Who will take care of the kids when I'm gone? I might never see them again. The world's so huge it could swallow them up. There's no map for where my father's headed.

A convertible stops and the driver leans toward me. He smiles but his eyes are like bullet holes. Empty.

"Looking for a ride?" he says. His tires are bald.

"Not really."

"Either you are or you aren't. You'll have to make up your mind." His smile smears across my body like oil.

I move back from the car. "I'm waiting for someone."

"Who?"

"My friend. He should be here any second."

"A friend, huh. That's one mighty lucky friend. Anyone ever tell you you're a pretty girl? Sexy, too, with that long, pretty hair and those long, sexy legs. They go all the way up?"

"Pardon?"

"I say, those legs go all the way up? Those are mighty sexy legs."

"I have to get going." But my body's frozen. What I see in those eyes has paralyzed me. He slides across the seat to the passenger side, stretching like a cat.

"Wait, what's the rush? Don't leave me, sweet thing. You sure you don't want a ride?"

"She's sure."

Daddy's behind me, holding the gun. He pulls bullets from his pocket and loads it. "My daughter and I are going to do some target shooting. She's a wonderful shot. Never misses. Want to see?"

"Hold on! I was just asking did she want a ride. She's standing by the road sticking out her thumb. What's a guy supposed to think?"

"A guy's supposed to leave while he's got the chance."

The convertible speeds off. Daddy looks at me sadly.

"I wouldn't have gone with him. His tires were bad." Then my arms are around him and I'm crying. "Daddy, I was scared! I didn't know what to do! I just stood there like an idiot!"

"Hush, now, baby. It's all right. Everything is going to be all right now." He holds me close and smoothes my hair. "I'm so sorry, Mary. It's all my fault. I'm so sorry about what happened. Seems like all I do is apologize lately. I should print up cards that say 'I'm sorry.' I could go around and hand them out." He examines my neck. "Did I hurt you?"

"It's okay."

"I don't know why I acted like that, Mary. I just went crazy. There's no excuse."

"So what were you going to do, shoot me?"

"What?" He remembers he's holding the gun. "No, I was going to practice for a while. Take out my frustrations on a helpless target. I mean it, honey. I'm so sorry, Mary. I promise I'll never hurt you again." His eyes gleam with tears. "Can you ever forgive me?"

I always forgive him. He's my father. I love him.

"Yes, Daddy. I'm sorry, too."

"Honey, you've got nothing to be sorry about. All you did was tell the truth. That's no crime. What happened in there was my fault, not yours. Sometimes I forget you're still a child."

"I don't feel like a child."

"That's my fault, too. Childhood's supposed to be a happy time. And it will be, soon, I swear it, Mary. I know I've said that before, but things are going to be different. When school starts this fall, you'll be there, I promise, sitting in the very front row. You're such a smart girl. Mama and I are so proud of you, honey. You know that, don't you?"

"I know it." My head's on his chest. I can hear his heart beating.

"You want to come and practice with me for a while?"

"The rangers said we're not supposed to shoot on the beach."

Daddy waves the gun impatiently. "It's not like we're hunting or endangering anybody. Those people on the ridge can't even hear us over the waves. They just don't want to share the beach. People are greedy, Mary, that's the trouble."

We cross the sand toward the cliffs, his arm around me.

"You were right about the house," he says. "You're always right. I didn't want the girls to know. It made them happy thinking we had someplace to go when our wandering days are over. It made me happy, too. I've been fooling myself, Mary, about so many things."

"When will they be over, Daddy? What are we going to do?"

"We'll go to San Francisco. I'll sell the RV. We won't get much for it; with the price of gas, nobody can afford to drive those things. But it'll be enough to rent a house and buy food until I'm working."

We reach the cliffs. The wind's knocked over the target. Daddy stands it up and hands me the gun. "You go first."

"I'll never be any good at this, Daddy."

"Of course you will. It just takes practice."

"But what's the point? I'd never use one of these things."

"Believe me, if you'd gotten in the car with that guy, you would've wished you'd had a gun. You would've used it. The most dangerous animal is a human being, especially when he's sick or hurt. Remember that, Mary. I keep trying to put that across to your mother. She says, 'Why can't people just be nice? What a wonderful world it would be.' That's true. But this isn't heaven; it's reality. She's never understood that, but you do."

He hands me the gun. I aim to please him, firing shot after shot at the target. His praise nourishes my hungry heart. It feels like the old days, father and daughter, not enemies enjoying an uneasy truce.

After a while he says, "You better go back and see how Mama's doing. She'll be worried about you."

I kiss his cheek and head up the beach. The roaring waves absorb the gun's report. I look back; Daddy has disappeared behind a rising wall of mist. The feel of his fingers on my throat has faded, too, like an old bruise, a bad dream. Once we're settled, that kind of stuff won't happen. It never used to happen before. We'll be happy again; a real family, living in a real house.

Inside the Wolfs' Den someone's playing my guitar.

I burst through the door; Danielle's got it on her lap and Polly's pulling on the strings. Andy's sitting on the floor, listening. Erica freezes when she sees me.

"What the hell are you doing?"

Danielle sticks out her chin. "Mama said we could."

"I don't care what she said. You're not supposed to touch it when I'm not here."

"This thing came off," Erica whispers.

"What thing?"

She reluctantly hands me one of the pegs.

"What happened?"

"We just turned it."

"Well, you turned it too hard! You broke it!" I snatch the guitar from Danielle.

Mama comes out of the bathroom, looking sheepish.

"I didn't think you'd mind. They were just playing with it, Mary."

"It's not a toy! Now it's broken. I can't tune it!"

"Just that one string."

"You need every string! You had no right to let them use it! It's not your guitar. It's mine!"

"Well, the girls were so upset after you and Daddy left. I thought it might calm them down."

I look in the guitar case. My secret money is gone.

"I had some money in here. Where is it?"

"I didn't take it," Erica says.

"Did you take it, Danielle?"

"There wasn't any money in there," she says, sneering.

"Yes there was. Now it's gone. Did you take it, Polly?"

"No."

"There wasn't any money in there," Mama says. "Just some picks and strings."

"Then where did it go?"

"I don't know," she says. "Maybe someone broke into the RV and stole it."

I search her face for clues. It's blank and smooth, as carefully arranged as a vase of flowers.

Fury sweeps over me, drenching my heart. I smash the guitar against the refrigerator. The body splinters, springs scream and sprawl. It dangles from my hand by its broken neck.

"She's crazy," Danielle says. Erica bursts into tears.

"Oh, Mary, why'd you have to do that?" Mama says sadly. "Now nobody can play with it."

Fifteen

"Mary, that boy's outside," Daddy said, sticking his head into the bathroom, where I was washing my face. I haul water from the faucet by the highway every morning. "Why's he coming around so early?"

"I don't know, Daddy."

"Tell him not to come around so early. Mama and the girls are still sleeping."

A thick mist was falling. Rocky was wearing a plastic trash bag, with holes cut out for his arms and head.

"Disposable clothing. What will they think of next?"

He smiled. "It works. I hope I didn't get you in trouble. I knocked real quiet in case no one was up."

"That's okay. What's happening?"

"I'm leaving."

"Now?" My heart contracted. I knew this was coming, but I wasn't ready. I wouldn't ever be ready to say good-bye.

"This morning. The carnival's getting into Cloverdale. I want to be there when they're hiring. I don't know what else to do. At least I'll have a job for a while and maybe get to travel around."

"Makes sense," I said. As much as anything did.

"Dave's taking some kids over to the carnival next week. Maybe you can come and I'll get to see you."

"We'll probably be gone by then," I said. "We're leaving as soon as the battery comes."

"That's what I figured." Rocky studied his feet. The toes of his shoes were freshly wrapped with duct tape.

"Are you leaving right away?"

"I've got to pack. Then I'll hitch a ride. It might take a while, so I want to get started."

"Want some company while you pack?"

"That'd be nice."

"How about breakfast?"

"Sure, if you can spare it. I don't want to mooch."

I went back into the RV and made peanut butter sandwiches and took a carton of orange juice out of the fridge.

Daddy looked up from his newspaper.

"Where are you going with that? I've told you we can't afford to feed him."

"This'll be the last time," I said. "He's leaving."

Daddy's face softened. "Where's he headed?"

"Cloverdale. There's a carnival coming. He's going to try to get hired."

"I'm sorry, honey. I know you'll miss him."

"It doesn't matter," I said. "We'll be leaving soon anyway."

"It matters." Daddy kissed my forehead. He took a ten dollar bill out of his wallet. "Give him this."

"Are you sure we can afford it?"

"He needs it more than we do. Take some cheese, too. There's plenty."

I slipped on my jacket and joined Rocky outside.

"My dad said to give you this."

"Ten bucks! Wow, I thought he didn't even like me."

"He does now," I said.

I sat in the doorway of his hut while he packed. It didn't take long. Soon his backpack was bulging. Then we sat on the tarp and ate breakfast.

"This is a pretty nice hut," he said. "Somebody will like it a lot."

"They'll think you did a good job of fixing it up."

"You can come down and hang around if you want, if the kids are bugging you or something."

"Yeah, maybe I'll come down here and smash up my guitar some more."

"You sure it can't be fixed?"

"You've seen it. It's shot. It's my own damn fault."

"Well, she shouldn't have let them play with it."

"Yeah, but I didn't need to go crazy."

"You were feeling a little tense."

"That's an understatement."

We make each other laugh. That's what I'll miss the most.

"You guys still going to San Francisco?"

"Far as I know. That's the plan. I'd just like to be somewhere long enough to finish school."

Rocky takes a drink of juice, then wipes his mouth. "I sure hope this carnival thing works out."

"What if it doesn't?"

"I'll find something else." He finishes his sandwich. "I'm sure going to miss you, Mary."

"Me, too. I mean, you. You're the first, you know, boyfriend I've ever had." I feel shy saying it out loud, but it's true. He's not just my friend, he's my boyfriend, too.

"I bet lots of boys liked you."

"I don't know. We moved so much. Nobody really got to know me."

"You're so pretty, Mary. I mean it. And you're the nicest girl I've ever met."

"And you're the nicest boy."

"What a coincidence," he says. We smile, then we're folded in each other's arms.

"I probably taste like peanut butter."

"You taste just fine. You're so sweet, Mary."

"I'm going to miss you, Rocky." I fight back tears, my shoulders shaking.

He hugs me tight. "You know what I wish? I wish I'd win the lottery. I'd buy your family a big house and get me one next door."

"Well, maybe you'll win sometime."

"I'm not old enough to play. But I will be, soon. He puts his hand on my chest. "I can feel your heart beating."

I put my hand on his chest. "I can feel yours, too."

We rest against each other. He says, "I hate to leave you."

"I know. When you go, I won't have anyone to talk to."

"Your family," he says.

"No, they think I'm too depressing."

"We can stay in touch. The trouble is, how? We'll both be moving around."

"I'll give you my aunt's address. She'll know where we are."

"That won't work. I'd probably lose it. Wait, I know." He digs a pen out of his knapsack.

"What's her phone number?"

I tell him and he writes it on his wrist.

"That'll wash off."

"No it won't. I'll touch it up every day."

"Now you've got a tattoo, the carnival will hire you for sure."

He smiles. "Well, I hate to say this, but I better get going. It might take a while to catch a ride." He hands me his flashlight. "I want you to keep this. Whenever you turn it on, think of me."

His words hang between us. Then we crack up.

"You know what I mean," he says, blushing.

"I sure do!"

"No, really. The batteries are almost new."

"Are you sure you won't need it?"

"I'm going to the big city, missy. There'll be lights and running water and all kinds of fancy things."

"All right," I say. "That's really nice. I wish I had something to give you, too."

"Don't worry, you've given me a lot," he says.

He folds up the tarp and ties it to his pack. We leave the hut and head toward the highway. Rocky looks back once.

I watch our feet plod across the sand, wishing I could turn them in another direction, back to the past, to the driftwood hut, to an unbroken moment of closeness and laughter. I don't even have a picture of Rocky. I burn his face into my memory.

We get to the highway and I sit on a big log next to City Hall.

"I'll keep you company till you get a ride."

"That could take some time."

"My schedule's not too full today."

Rocky walks over to the road and sticks out his thumb.

"I don't think you need to do that until cars go by."

"I know," he says. "I'm just practicing."

A couple of cars pass, packed with families. Kids hang out the windows, gawking at Rocky. Another car pulling a trailer speeds by.

"How'm I doing?"

"Not too good. Do you think wearing a trash bag has something to do with it?"

"I need a sign. That would help."

"You could write it on your arm."

"Then people would really think I'm crazy."

Another car approaches and slows down; then the driver checks out Rocky and keeps going.

"Boy, talk about an anticlimax," I say. "You're supposed to kiss me and ride off into the sunset."

"I'm trying, I'm trying. Geez, my thumb is getting tired."

"You could hold up your leg."

"Yeah, maybe a dog would stop."

We keep waiting and waiting.

"This could take all day," he says.

"I hope not. The suspense is killing me. I don't want to have to keep saying good-bye."

"I'll never forget you, Mary."

"You better not. Get ahold of my aunt in a while. She'll know where we are. I'll let her know you'll be calling."

"That'd be good. Otherwise she might think I'm some nut who's bothering you."

"She would if she could see you right now."

"It's just a trash bag, for God's sake! It's keeping me dry."

"You should write that on a sign. People probably think you escaped from the dump."

A pickup passes him, then stops and backs up. The driver's long hair is tied with a bandanna. Two smiling women sit beside him. They unroll the window and music blares out.

The driver leans toward Rocky. "Where you headed, man?"

"Cloverdale."

"Nobody goes to Cloverdale," one of the women says, giggling.

"I can give you a ride to the junction; then I'm headed south."

"That's fine. I'll take it."

"You'll have to ride in back, man. There's no room up front. Sorry."

"No problem." Rocky tosses his knapsack in the bed of the truck and climbs in, sitting with his back against the cab.

"Maybe I'll see you next week," he tells me.

"Maybe. Take care. I'll be seeing you, Rocky."

"That's for sure." He holds up his tattooed wrist. "This arm is sacred. I'll never wash it."

"I'll remember that the next time you hug me."

The truck pulls onto the highway, spitting gravel from the tires. The tires aren't bad. He'll be okay. He salutes me with his tattooed arm. I turn on the flashlight and wave it back and forth until the truck rounds a curve and Rocky's gone.

Sixteen

Two days later the rangers came by and told us the county was closing the beach and everybody had to leave.

"How much time have we got?" Daddy asked them.

"Hard to say," Rita said. "Couple of weeks, couple of months. Depends how much pressure they're getting from the top."

"Those people up there?" Daddy aimed his eyes at the ridge.

"No, the state," Rita said, but he wasn't listening.

"I'd like to show those people what pressure feels like. Let them see how it feels at the bottom. Bunch of rich bastards, think they're better than everyone."

"Come on, Andrew," Tom said. "You knew this was coming."

The news thundered through the campground. People swarmed around Daddy like frightened children in a storm, begging him for shelter, for answers.

"Andrew, what are we going to do, man?" Dave asked. "Maybe you should call the TV people, or we could do that other stuff you said."

"I don't know what you're going to do," Daddy told him, "but as soon as the battery comes, we're leaving."

The crowd buzzed, shocked. People looked puzzled, lost.

"What about the lawyer?" Janice asked. "You said we could get a lawyer to help us."

"Maybe you can, but we're moving on. I've got a job waiting in San Francisco. I talked to them this morning. They want me down there right away. I wish I could stay and help you."

Dave looked stunned, but he patted Daddy's shoulder. "No, man, it's okay. You gotta do what you gotta do. We'll go up and get that battery tomorrow."

"You said we could fight it." Janice's voice was shrill. "You said you were going to help us."

Daddy got angry, too. "Hey, look: I'm not God. I'm not the Wizard of Oz. What do you expect me to do?"

"I expect you to do what you said you'd do! You're just like those people up there! You've got yours and the hell with everybody else!"

"Honey, don't," Dave said. "It's not his fault." She leaned against him, sobbing. He led her away.

Daddy went into the RV and opened a beer. "Christ, I'll be so glad to get out of here," he said.

Daddy and I installed the new battery the next morning, but the engine wouldn't turn over. It didn't even whimper. Daddy raged around the RV, punching and kicking it. Mama stood on the steps, drying her hands with a dish towel, afraid to ask him what was wrong.

"Acting like that won't do any good," I said.

"Oh, really? Thanks for pointing that out."

"Being sarcastic won't help either."

"I don't think you appreciate our situation, Mary. We've got to get this thing running. We've got to get out of here!"

He looked like he wanted to smash the windshield, finishing the job the crack had started.

"Maybe it's the plugs."

"It's not the plugs. They're almost new."

"Well, it's got to be something."

"That's brilliant, Mary. Let me jot that down."

"Don't take it out on me! It's not my fault!"

"Are you sure you put it in right?" Mama ventured timidly. "Maybe some of the wires got crossed."

Daddy stared at her incredulously. "Speaking of crossed wires, since when are you an expert on the RV? Butt out and let me handle this, Wendy."

"I'm just saying—"

"Don't say anything at all."

"Andrew, you shouldn't talk to me like that." She stuck out her chin, but her voice trembled.

"I don't want to talk to you at all right now. Just get out of here and let me think."

"I'm not a child—"

"Get out of here, I said!"

She withdrew inside the Wolfs' Den and slammed the door.

"I hate it when you act like that," I said.

He sat beside me on the ground and rubbed his face, smearing engine oil across his chin.

"You're right. I'm a jerk. I apologize. Does everyone hear me? I apologize! I apologize for everything, whatever it is! The thing is, Mary, I'm not a magician. Whatever goes wrong, she expects me to fix it. The RV won't run? Here's a new engine! We need more money? Here's a thousand up my sleeve! Well, Andrew Wolf's bag of tricks is empty, as empty as his goddamn wallet."

"Dave might know what's wrong. He knows a lot about cars."

But Dave didn't know what was wrong with the RV. He and Louie and Abalone John spent hours under the engine hood. Mama brought out potato chips and beer. Daddy whispered in her ear and nuzzled her cheek. She accepted his kisses and apology and took Andy and the girls to the beach.

Dave shook his head. "I don't know what's wrong with this thing. I've never worked on this kind of motor before."

"We could ask Big Ed," Abalone John said.

Daddy shook his head. "He's crazy."

"He may be strange but he knows engines," Dave said. "He had his own shop in the East Bay."

"If he's so good, what's he doing here?"

"Let's put it this way: He had some problem with the boys."

"The boys?"

"He used to be a Hell's Angel."

"So?"

"It was a bad deal or something. Maybe he narced on them, I don't know. I don't want to know. All I know is, he can't go back. There's people looking for him and it ain't the cops."

"No, I don't want him around here," Daddy said.

"You want this rig running? You want to get out of here? It can't hurt to ask him."

"You ask him," Daddy said.

Dave limped off toward Big Ed's hut. He came back alone.

"He's coming," Dave said. "He was taking a nap."

"Getting his beauty rest," Louie said.

"Mary, go inside."

"Daddy, he's not going to eat me."

"You never know," Louie said. Abalone John

laughed. I stayed where I was, on the RV's steps. I was curious to see the man up close.

In a while Big Ed loomed across the sand.

"Geez, he's bigger than God," John whispered.

The sun was hot but Big Ed wore leather, black pants and a vest over his matted chest. His enormous boots were draped with chains. His long hair was stiff with sweat.

"What's the problem?" he growled.

"We don't know," Daddy said. "It just won't start. Care for a beer?" Daddy tossed him a can and Big Ed drained it, a trickle cutting through his tangled beard.

"Got any more?"

I brought out another can and handed it to him. He smelled powerfully of feet and gasoline. Big Ed emptied and dropped the can. Dave picked it up and put it in his vest pocket.

"Got a cigarette?"

Dave gave him one, then lit one for himself and offered me the pack.

"I quit," I told him. "It didn't make me feel too good."

"That's funny." Dave pretended to cough up his lungs. "It makes me feel like a million bucks."

"Green and wrinkled," Louie added, lighting up. Big Ed got under the hood with his cigarette. It seemed dangerous but nobody mentioned it.

Big Ed tugged on wires. He sniffed the

engine. He plucked out the battery and asked for a wrench.

"What's wrong? Did they sell me a crummy battery? Maybe the battery's no good," Daddy said. "Is that the problem?" Big Ed ignored him. Dave signaled Daddy not to bug him.

Big Ed straightened up and wiped his hands on his pants.

"Thirsty," he said, looking at me.

I brought out another beer. He gulped it down and belched. Dave offered him the pack of cigarettes. He kept it.

"Can you see anything wrong? What's the problem?" Daddy asked. "Is there a problem with the battery?"

"Head's cracked," Big Ed said, looking bored.

"What's that mean?"

"Means you're fucked. Look at here." Big Ed pointed with the wrench. "See this? The head's cracked."

"Can't it be fixed?"

The biker looked at Daddy as if he were stupid. "Yeah, with a new one."

"Andrew, it needs a new engine," Dave explained gently.

Daddy sagged. "That'll cost a fortune."

"You got it." Big Ed nodded. "Coupla thousand, at least."

"A couple of thousand! I don't have a coupla thousand!"

Big Ed shrugged. "You don't have a engine, either. What you got is a piece of shit on wheels."

Daddy's eyes bulged. The cords on his neck stood out. I was afraid he was going to start shouting.

Dave read the signs, too. He shook Big Ed's hand and walked him away. "Thanks for coming down here, Ed. We really appreciate it. I'll come by later and bring that fish."

"You won't forget?" It wasn't a question.

"No way. I'll be there."

"Bring plenty," Big Ed said.

The men watched him go, then crowded around my father, murmuring words of sympathy, as if a family member had died.

"Man, what a bummer," Abalone John said.

"Tough break, Andrew," Louie said. "What're you going to do now?"

"I don't know." Daddy sounded vague, as if he wasn't following the conversation.

"Andrew, it's not the end of the world, man," Dave said. "Everything that's broken can be fixed."

"Not without money."

"You'll get the money. There's no sense beating yourself up over this thing."

I wasn't worried about Daddy beating himself up. I was worried about what would happen to us when the men went home.

"Well, I gotta go catch some fish for Ed," Dave said. "Let's hope they'll bite, or he will."

"Thanks," Daddy said. "Thanks for everything."

"Hey, no problem. That's what friends are for."

Daddy grabbed Dave's arm. "Maybe he's wrong about the engine. Are you sure he knows what he's talking about?"

"Only when it comes to motors and drugs. Take it easy, Andrew. It'll be all right."

"Don't let it get you down," Louie added, walking away.

Mama and the kids were coming up from the beach. They waved at Daddy. He just looked at them blankly, as if they were strangers, shadows.

He's acting differently than I thought he would. Not breaking things, not shouting. He's sitting in the driver's seat, staring out the window, as if he's traveling on an unpaved road through country he's never seen.

Mama put the girls to bed right after supper.

"Daddy's tired," she explained. They didn't complain; they could feel the tide of tension rising.

He wouldn't eat dinner. He's been drinking brandy. He keeps it in his bedside drawer, with the gun. I was afraid he'd notice the gun was gone, but he was in a hurry for the bottle.

He wouldn't, you know, hurt anyone, but he might get mad and go up on the ridge and wave the gun around. If they had guns, too, something bad might happen. Besides, I was scared one of the kids would find it. They're supposed to stay out of that drawer, but kids do stupid things. They forget. I've begged him to leave the gun unloaded. He won't.

"What good would that do in an emergency? What would I say: 'Please wait here, Mr. Psycho, while I find my bullets'? Nuts aren't especially cooperative, Mary. That's what makes them nuts."

"Kids aren't especially cooperative either. That's what makes them kids."

He never listens. So I hid the gun this afternoon, when Dave and the others left. It's under the RV. Daddy hasn't missed it. He just wanted that bottle of brandy.

Now it's empty.

"We got something else?" he asks Mama. "Beer?"

"It's gone."

"All gone. And no place to rest his weary head."

"I can run down and see if Dave and Janice have something."

"Yes! Why don't you do that? Why don't you run down there on your chubby little legs and see? He better have something. It's the least he can do."

Mama hands Andy to me and leaves. He's wide-awake and waving a rattle.

"It's not Dave's fault the engine's shot," I say. "He was just trying to help."

"By bringing that stinking cretin here to drink all my beer and insult me? He's probably lying about the engine, telling me it's junk so he can buy it himself and sell it."

"I doubt it. How many miles do we have on it, anyway?"

"Millions. Billions. You're probably right. But then, you always are, aren't you, Mary?" He's looking for a villain, a victim, a fight.

"Getting drunk won't help."

"Right again! Right as rain! To think I've raised such a brilliant child, who can point out every time I'm wrong, which happens hundreds of times each day. I'm always wrong and you're always right! What a perfect arrangement!"

"I can't talk to you when you're like this," I say. I'd like to tell him he's acting like an idiot, but I can feel the girls listening, holding their breath.

"Mary," he says, stumbling over to me and Andy, "do you have any idea what it's like to be me? To be in the middle of this godawful mess? My life—" He gropes for words, shakes his head. "I look in the mirror some mornings, Mary, and I can't believe what I'm seeing. I can't believe it's really me. I look out the window and I think I'm dreaming, but no matter what I do, I can't wake up. Do you understand what I'm telling you."

"Yes."

"No you don't. You're just nodding your head. How could you know? You're still a child. Have you ever known me to drink to excess? To shirk my responsibilities? And now you're calling me an alcoholic—"

"No I'm not. I'm just saying that getting drunk won't help."

"But there you're wrong. See, you're wrong sometimes, Mary." He sits heavily beside me. Andy reaches up and grabs his nose. "Without the liquid strength from that bottle, I'd never have the courage to do what must be done."

"What's that?"

"I'm going to ask dear old dad for a loan."

"I don't think that's such a good idea." Grampa hung up on him the last time he called.

"Then what would you suggest? Should I rob a bank? Should I try to sell this little boy? This is a crisis. This is an emergency, Mary. I don't think you fully grasp our predicament. We've reached the end of the line here."

"You could call Aunt Belle. She'd send us the money."

He laughs. "Wouldn't she love to hear me squirm."

"She's not like that. You know she loves you."

"She loves the person I used to be. I'm not that person anymore."

"Yes you are. You've just had some bad luck."

"Mary, you should be a diplomat. You're wasting your talents here. I'm serious, you should work for the U.N." He returns to the bottle, then remembers it's empty. "Wendy! Where'd that woman go?"

"She went to Dave's, to get you something to drink."

"Mary, your mother is a wonderful woman. She deserves so much better than this, than me." He looks out at the night through the open door. "I don't know what I'd do if she ever left me."

"She's not going to leave you. Nobody's leaving you. Everything's going to be fine. We'll figure this out."

"There's nothing to figure out," he says flatly. "We've got to get some money. I'll call my father."

"Maybe you better not do it tonight."

"Why not? Are you afraid he'll be able to tell that I'm tipsy? Let him see what he's driven me to! Is this any way for a man to treat his children? Would I turn you away if you asked me for help? Would I turn away that beautiful little boy?"

"I'll call, if you want. I'll talk to Grampa."

He shakes his head violently. "Absolutely not. I got us into this and I'll get us out. Then we'll go down to the city and I'll get a job—" He winces and clutches his belly.

"What's the matter? Your stomach again? You've got to see a doctor."

179

"Good idea. We'll go to the Mayo Clinic tomorrow. I'll fly us there in my private jet."

Mama comes in waving a small bottle of vodka as if it's a winning lottery ticket.

"Dave says he's sorry this is all he has."

"The man is a prince. Do we have any mixer?"

She's looking in the fridge. "Just milk."

Daddy laughs as if she's a great comedian. "Just give me some ice cubes in a glass."

She fixes the drink and he sips it, smiling. Mama sits next to me and nurses Andy. He lifts a tiny hand and pats her cheek.

"Could there be anything more beautiful than that sight?" Daddy says. "I am a man truly blessed. I love you, Wendy. You know that, don't you?"

"Of course I do, darling. And I love you."

"And I love you, Mary. I really do. Even though we argue sometimes. I want you to know I still respect your opinion."

The storm has passed. The girls breathe deeply, sleeping. Outside a dog barks; then the beach is peaceful.

My father finishes his drink. "I better make that call."

"What call?" Mama asks.

He stands, almost losing his balance. "I'm throwing myself on the mercy of the court. In other words, I'm calling my father."

"It's kind of late," I say. "Maybe you should wait until tomorrow."

"Mary, never put off until tomorrow what you can put off for the rest of your life. Unfortunately, this can't be avoided any longer." He stumbles toward the door. Mama signals me with her eyes.

"I'll come with you, Daddy. I'll bring my flashlight."

I'm thinking of you, Rocky, as I turn it on. Daddy clutches my arm, tripping over rocks.

"A sign of old age. No night vision. Whatever you do, Mary, don't get old."

"Are you sure you don't want me to call?"

"What's the matter? Don't you think I can handle it?"

"No, it's just—"

"What's the number, Mary? My mind's gone blank."

I dial the number and hand him the phone. Grandma answers. Grampa never talks unless he has to.

"Oh, we're fine," Daddy's saying. "You should see the baby. We're going to come back when I take my vacation."

I tune him out. He's telling her a story, the story I've heard so many times before, where everybody lives happily ever after.

But first, a word from our sponsor.

"Well, I know that," he's saying, "and I

appreciate that, Mother, but I didn't plan for the engine to break. It's just one of those things. . . . I understand that, Mother. Well, of course I'll talk to him. That's why I'm calling."

I try not to listen but I can't help it.

"Dad! It's good to hear your voice. How are you doing? Oh, we're just fine."

Couldn't be better. Except for one tiny problem. But everything's going to be different this time; he's got a wonderful job, he's making tons of money, he'll pay Grampa back right away, wait and see.

"Well, I can't just sell it." Daddy's getting loud. "Nobody's going to buy it in this condition. It's not running, that's the point. Aren't you listening to me?"

Then Grampa's talking, his voice squawking out of the receiver. A car on the highway splashes light on Daddy's face. Grampa would be scared if he could see it. I look away.

"I understand that, Dad, but you don't— Listen to me! You don't understand the situation we're in. I'm not asking for myself. I'm talking about your grandchildren!"

It quickly gets worse. "I am not 'holding them hostage to get to you'! What kind of man do you think I am?"

My grandfather tells him. Daddy shouts into the phone.

"Well, you won't have to worry about that

anymore! Forget it! Forget the whole damn thing!"

He smashes the receiver against the phone booth and hangs up so hard it falls and dangles.

He collapses, sobbing. "Mary, he hates me! My own father hates me!"

"No he doesn't, Daddy." I've got my arm around him, trying to sit him up.

"He thinks I'm a liar! You know what he said? He thinks I'm spending the money on drugs! That's a laugh! I wish I were on drugs! Then I wouldn't know what's happening."

"Daddy, he just doesn't understand."

"The hell with all of them! I'm never going back there! They'll never see you kids again! We don't need them. We'll make it on our own. I'll just, I'll just— What am I going to do? Mary, what am I going to do? Please help me!"

"Don't worry, Daddy. I'll call Aunt Belle."

He pushes me away. "And have her laugh in my face?"

"She wouldn't laugh at you."

"Did you hear what I said? I'm the boss here, Mary."

I help him to his feet. We head back to the campground.

Mama looks up anxiously as we come in.

"How'd it go?" She sees his face. "What's wrong? What happened?"

"Selfish pig! He'll be sorry about that.

They're never going to see us again. The man has no feeling for his own flesh and blood! Mary can tell you. She heard it, she knows. Mary was there. She can tell you."

"Maybe you can talk to your mother," Mama says.

"That won't do any good. He's the big cheese, you know. She's just his puppet, his slave. It's always been like this, ever since we were kids. My sister was always their favorite."

"So what're we going to do?" Mama whispers.

"We're going to do what we should've done a long time ago. We're going to the county and get on welfare. Why the hell should all these foreigners get food stamps and rent and help for their children when the people who live here, the goddamn citizens, work their butts off for years like a bunch of idiots and get treated like dogs, get nothing? I've paid my taxes, now I want my share and they better not give me any bullshit, I've had it."

Mama looks so relieved it almost breaks my heart. It's Christmas Eve and Santa Claus is coming.

Daddy says, "Is the vodka gone?"

"No, there's some left. Do you want it with milk?"

She's trying to make him smile, but he's not listening. He sits behind the steering wheel, staring out the windshield, his finger tapping and tapping his lips.

Seventeen

Mama was supposed to go to the welfare office with Daddy, but she said she had a terrible headache.

"Don't give me that," he said.

"My head is killing me!"

"Get out of that bed."

"I won't!" Mama said.

Daddy grabbed her arm and tugged. He barely budged her.

"Daddy, stop!" Erica cried. "You're hurting Mama!"

Andy turned his head to watch them. The cereal I was feeding him grazed his cheek.

"Get out of that bed this minute!" Daddy said. He tore the blankets out of her fingers.

"My head is splitting! You don't know how I feel!"

"How do you think I feel, Wendy? Do you

think I want to go down there today and tell them I'm forty-two years old and I got squat?"

"Don't talk like that," Mama said. "Just because we live here doesn't mean you need to sound like a redneck."

"What an amazing coincidence that you have a headache this morning. You'll probably feel better this afternoon." Daddy crossed his arms. "We'll wait."

"You should go early. You don't have an appointment."

"No, we'll go when your headache's gone."

"You're procrastinating," Mama said.

"You're lying there like a beached whale telling me I'm procrastinating?"

"Don't call me a whale!"

"Then get out of that bed!"

Danielle ate her cereal, looking disgusted. She hardly speaks to any of us lately. Since I smashed up my guitar she thinks I'm crazy. Maybe she's right. I sure miss playing, getting lost in the music inside my head.

"I'll get you some aspirin," Daddy said.

"Aspirin won't help."

"How do you know?"

"I tried it! I was up all night!"

"That's funny, I was up, too and I never saw you!"

"You guys," I said. "You should hear yourselves. You sound like a couple of morons."

They looked as if they might get mad at me, and then they started giggling. Daddy sat next to Mama on the bed.

"But honey," he said, "if you don't come with me, maybe they won't believe that I have a wife and children."

"Of course they will. Someone comes out and makes a home visit. Today you'll just fill out an application."

"How do you know?"

"A little bird told me."

"A little bird named Janice? She's not on welfare," Daddy said. Dave gets money from the service and disability.

"No, but she knows the ropes."

"I think you know the ropes, too, lady. Better than Houdini himself." Daddy bent down and kissed her. She ruffled his hair.

"They're nuts," Danielle muttered.

"I'll go with you, Daddy," I said. "I'll take Andy with me so Mama can rest."

Mama batted her eyelashes and clasped her hands to her breast. "Really? I feel better already."

"It's a miracle!" Daddy pinched her belly. She screeched. "You can come, Mary, but we can't take Andy. We might get hung up there all day."

"I'll bring bottles for him. Don't worry, he'll be fine."

I had a plan. While Daddy filled out the

application, I'd take Andy to the free clinic. Maybe he could get his vaccinations. Once it was done, Mama and Daddy wouldn't mind. Some of the kids around here aren't too healthy.

"Better leave him," Mama said regretfully. "He might fuss."

"This good boy? This good boy won't fuss." I nuzzled Andy's neck until he squealed.

"Well, I guess it's all right."

"Take me, too!" Polly begged.

"Not today, honey. Next time," I promised. "But I'll bring you something."

"Like what? A toy?"

"How about ice cream?"

"Oh boy!" She clapped her hands. "Mary's going to bring us some ice cream!"

"Big wow," Danielle said, stomping outside.

While Mama got Andy ready, I ran down to Dave's. He'd agreed to loan us his car. I parked it beside the RV and got out. Danielle was chucking rocks at the ground.

"What if they won't help us?" she said.

"They will." We have no money, no car, no jobs. We've got everything going for us: nothing. "Don't worry, things are under control."

"It sure didn't sound that way last night. You guys think I'm sleeping but I'm not; I hear you." She was trying to look tough, her eyes mean and squinty.

"Daddy was all worked up, but everything's

fine now." I put my hand on her arm but she shrugged it off.

"You're a liar. You guys are a bunch of liars."

"Don't call me a liar."

"Then don't act like one. Why'd you say he sold the house that time?"

"Because he did. It's the truth."

"He didn't! I asked him."

"When?"

"That day, after you ran out."

"He said I was lying?"

"Why'd you lie about the house?"

I was drowning in her words, in the hate in her eyes. I thought he had finally told them the truth. Suddenly I felt so tired, as if all the life had leaked out of me.

"Believe whatever you want, Danielle. I guess you'll have to figure it out."

"Some choice." She threw a fistful of rocks onto the ground. "Liar. You're just a bunch of liars."

I went into the RV and picked up Andy. I got his changing bag and put his stroller over my arm. They I went out and sat in the passenger seat. I couldn't even look at my father.

"Beautiful day," he said as we drove down the highway. The windows won't roll up, so he talked loud. "Look at that cloud. What's it look like to you?"

"Rain."

"No! A cow. See, there's the head, and there's the tail on the other end. What's the matter with you, Mary? You're awfully quiet."

"I guess I don't have much to say."

He was enjoying the drive, the feeling of freedom. He listened to a talk show on the radio. Andy doesn't have a car seat, so he sat on my lap, the seat belt stretched tight across us.

After a while Daddy remembered where we were headed. "I hope this goes all right today. How do I look?"

"Fine." He was wearing his best shirt and pants and had touched up his shoes with black crayon.

"It's just as well your mother didn't come. These things have to be handled with finesse. You don't want to lie, but you can't exactly tell the truth. If you do, you'll just screw yourself up. It's a shame, but that's how the game is played. Your mother can't do it; she's too honest."

"Hmmm."

"We're not asking for a handout; just a helping hand. Some people make a career out of standing in line. I'm not talking about the ones who need help. That's different. But if they don't want to work or they're on drugs or something, the hell with them."

"What if they have kids?"

He shot me a look.

"You can't punish the kids because the parents are jerks."

"Why are you arguing with me, Mary?"

"I'm not."

"Why do you always have to argue?"

"I'm not! I'm just saying it's complicated. Maybe we won't even qualify. You should've called and asked."

"They brush you off on the phone. Any fool knows that. You have to go down there in person. What are you saying? That I'm some freeloading bum? I've never asked for a dime in my life!"

"I'm just saying there's rules. Rules change all the time."

"Then they can change them for us! We're not some scum they can kick under the desk and ignore. This is a special situation."

"Not to them."

"Janice thinks we'll qualify."

"Janice thinks Elvis is alive and well. Maybe he'll loan us some money."

"What's the matter with you? Whose side are you on?"

"I'm just pointing out some facts."

"I'll point out the facts. When we get there, you just keep your mouth shut and let me do the talking." Daddy sighed. "Who would've thought it would come to this? It's funny how things turn out."

"Hilarious."

"If somebody had told me I'd be on welfare someday, I would've said they were crazy. Don't worry, it's only till we get on our feet. Sometimes a man has to swallow his pride. But I'll tell you, Mary, I'm choking on this thing. If it weren't for your mother and you kids, I'd tell these people to go to hell."

"That'd go over good." Andy nibbled on my thumb. His bottom teeth are coming in. "How much do you think they'll give us?"

"Whatever it is, it won't be enough, but it's more than we've got right now," he said.

"Watch that truck." We were closer to the city. The traffic on the highway was thick and fast.

"Mary, do you mind? I've been driving half my life."

"Not lately, and not in the city," I said. "I think you're supposed to take the next exit."

"I can read, too. Will you relax?"

We got lost downtown in a maze of one-way streets. It wasn't a hot day, but Daddy was sweating. We stopped at a gas station so I could ask directions while Daddy jiggled Andy on his lap.

The county complex was huge. We drove in circles, looking for the Department of Social Services. Daddy got madder and madder.

"Look at the size of this place," he fumed. "It's like Disneyland for bureaucrats. This is why we don't have any money, Mary. The government keeps getting bigger and bigger and the people keep getting smaller."

"There's Social Services. It's that big pink building."

The lots were full. We had to park far away.

"What do we do now, call a cab?" Daddy grumbled. He combed his hair and put on his sports coat. I unfolded Andy's stroller and strapped him in. He smiled at us and waved his arms and legs.

We walked back to Social Services. The waiting room was jammed with men and women, mostly women, and bored, restless kids bugging their mothers and each other. Several long lines snaked slowly toward counters where employees dispensed answers and applications.

My father went up to the information window, where a man was arguing with a clerk.

"I understand that, sir," the clerk was saying as if she'd said it a million times that day.

"You understand nothing. You're not listening to me."

"Excuse me," Daddy said, "I just need to know—"

"I'm sorry, sir, you'll have to wait your turn," the clerk said.

"No cuts," the man behind Daddy muttered.

"I just want to know if I'm in the right line."

"You'll have to wait your turn, sir, like everybody else."

Daddy got in line behind the others. "This is going to take all day," he said.

"We'll walk around. I'll check back later."

I wheeled Andy out the door and past the courthouse. There were policemen outside, and lots of worried-looking people. Two women who looked like secretaries walked by. One smiled at Andy, but the other one said, "Babies having babies" as they passed us.

The free clinic was full of women and kids. I got in the long line. It was finally our turn.

"Excuse me," I said to the woman at the counter. "Is this where people can get free shots?"

"For you or him?"

"Him. He needs his vaccinations."

"Are you on Medi-Cal?"

"No."

"Take a seat. You'll have to wait."

"I can't stay long. I have to catch my ride."

"Can you come back tomorrow?"

"No, we're just passing through."

Andy started fussing. I gave him a bottle of juice.

"How old is he?"

"Four months."

"And he hasn't had his shots?"

"No. We've been on the road for a while. I want to get it done right away."

"Wait here." The woman walked to a nearby desk and spoke to another woman.

"All right," she said when she came back, "but next time you'll have to wait your turn."

"Thanks. I really appreciate it."

She pulled out a form. "I need some information. Whose child is this?"

"Mine," I said.

Daddy wasn't in the car or the waiting room. I figured he was in an inner office, filling out his application. I took Andy to the ladies' room and changed his diaper and peeled the tiny bandage off his arm.

We strolled up and down the hallways, killing time, stopping in front of a door marked CHILD PROTECTIVE SERVICES.

I circled the waiting room, studying the posters as if they were exhibits in a museum. Then I found myself standing at the front counter, where a woman with short hair was talking on the phone.

"Sorry to keep you waiting," she said when she hung up. "How can I help you?"

"I was just kind of curious what you do here. I mean, is this where you go about child abuse?"

"This is the place. Did you want to make a report?"

"No. I was just wondering how you know if a child's being abused. I mean, when it's bad enough to do something."

She studied me, her face full of questions. I emptied my mind until my eyes were windows into windows.

"It depends. If it's physical abuse, there might be bruises or lacerations. If it's sexual abuse—"

"Oh, it's nothing like that. These kids aren't being hit or anything."

"Are they being neglected?"

"What do you mean by neglected?"

"Are their parents taking care of them? Do they have enough food and clothing?"

"Well, yeah. Their parents really love them. It's just, you know, a difficult situation."

"What seems to be the problem?"

"No problem," I said. "It's just that they don't have a place to stay."

"I see. Well, there's a homeless shelter downtown."

"They're not exactly homeless. Anyway, they're going on welfare. Just until they get on their feet."

"Well, if you feel it's a situation we should check out—"

"Oh, no, I was just curious," I said.

She handed me a card. "Call this number anytime. It's answered twenty-four hours a day."

"That's okay. I won't need it."

"Take it," she said. "Just in case."

When I got outside, I threw the card away.

Daddy's pacing in the hall in front of Social Services, his sports coat flapping he's moving so fast.

"I'm sorry we're late. I had to change Andy's diaper."

He marches toward the car. I can barely keep up. Andy's head bobs and the stroller rattles.

"I lost track of the time. I didn't mean to keep you waiting."

I'm talking to his back. He's almost running.

We get in the car and he slams the door, gripping the steering wheel, his chest heaving.

"I'm sorry, Daddy. I didn't think you'd be done so soon."

"They turned me down," he says.

"What?"

"You heard me!" he explodes. "Are you deaf? Are you stupid? They turned me down!"

"Why?"

He grinds the ignition and slams the car into reverse. We peel out of the parking lot, tires shrieking.

"They changed the rules! You're always right, aren't you, Mary? What's it like to always be right? They said, once you have a house, come back and we'll help you. Once I have a house I won't need their help! How am I supposed to get a house with no money? Has the world gone insane? Doesn't anybody listen?"

"Are you sure that's what they said? It doesn't make any sense."

"Of course it doesn't make sense! That's the government!" he shouts. "I tried to explain. This

197

is a special situation! I'm not like these people with their hands out all the time. They wouldn't listen to me! You should've seen their faces! Like I'm the scum of the earth, some worthless bum! Asking me all these stupid questions—"

"Did you answer the questions? You have to answer the questions."

"They want you down on your knees, they want you crawling like a dog. They threw me out in front of all those people! Everyone was laughing at me!"

He speeds down the street, cutting blindly through traffic. Horns are screaming. He screams back. I want to beg him to slow down but my tongue is frozen. Andy whimpers and hides his face against my neck.

We hurl along the ribbon of Highway 1, tires screeching on the curves, almost flying. Beside me, my father is making sounds like an animal caught in the jaws of a trap. Far below us, the restless ocean glitters like the fan of silver water he jumped through to please me, a lifetime ago. We laughed so hard. Now he's someone I don't know. He's like one of those animals you see on the road, that's been run over so many times you can't even tell what it was.

Eighteen

Sometimes that night we didn't understand what he was saying. He seemed to be arguing with people in his head, answering their accusations, seeing their laughing faces in the windshield.

He clutched the steering wheel of our dead RV as if he could lift it with the force of his will and fly it through the clouds, back home to Nebraska, back to the wrong turn in the road that led us here. Mama tiptoed through the Wolfs' Den like a grieving ghost, keeping the children away from him.

When he and Mama were in bed, I heard her say, "Now you'll have to call your sister." My father answered her with silence.

I lay in my bunk, listening to Mama cry, feeling Daddy's eyes burning up the darkness. When he finally fell asleep, I slipped out.

I found my way down the beach with

Rocky's flashlight. The hut was cold but I'd brought a blanket, and after a while I fell asleep. I dreamed we were back home, at our house in Nebraska. I was playing on the lawn. Daddy stepped through the sprinkler. He opened his briefcase; tons of money fell out. *Mary*, he said, *I almost forgot; I had this in my other wallet.*

When I woke up, I didn't know where I was. Fog draped the sun; the light was dim. The hut felt different with Rocky gone. But I imagined I could fell him there, his love reaching out to warm me.

I'll ask Aunt Belle to help us. She'll send us money to come home. Daddy will be furious, but there's no other way. His pride is like a big rock blocking the road.

I've drifted off again. Someone's calling my name.

I'm awake, Mama. I don't want to miss the school bus.

But Dave's in my dream, calling, "Mary, Mary!"

I open my eyes and crawl out of the hut.

He's limping across the sand, his bad leg swinging. "Mary, your father—" His face is wild. He's gasping for breath, his hands on his knees. "Your father's got a gun—"

"No, I hid it." It was there last night. There's no way he could've found it.

"He took one of mine. He's shooting up the RV. Mary, he's gone crazy. You've got to come!"

We run across the sand toward the campground.

"I called the sheriff," Dave says. They're on their way. They're sending the ambulance."

"Why?"

"He's got the girls in there with him, and your mother, Mary. I tried to get in but he wouldn't let me." Dave sobs, tears streaming down his cheeks.

We get to the Wolfs' Den. People watch from a distance, crouching behind cars and trailers.

"Just talk to him," Dave says. "He might listen to you."

"I'm going in."

Dave grabs my arm. "You can't! He might shoot you."

Has Dave gone crazy, too? "He'd never do that."

"I'm telling you, you can't go in there! It's not safe!"

"He's my father."

"Listen to me, Mary! He's not your father right now! I've seen this kind of thing before. There's no telling what he'll do!"

"I'll be okay." I turn away from Dave and reach under the RV. Then I call, "It's me, Daddy. Mary. I'm coming in."

I open the door and step inside. My eyes can't comprehend what they're seeing. Daddy's in back, by his bunk, holding a gun. Mama's facedown on the floor at his feet. I can't tell if she's breathing.

The girls sit on Danielle's bunk, faces white as their nightgowns, silent as a row of those wooden dolls that fit inside each other. Andy's on the floor beside my mother. He holds out his arms to me.

"Mary, I couldn't find you." Daddy looks relieved to see me, as if I've woken him from a terrible dream.

"I went down to Rocky's hut."

"How's he doing?"

"He's gone. Remember, he went to Cloverdale."

"That's right." He nods.

"What're you doing, Daddy?" My voice is calm, screams are clawing at the back of my teeth.

He spreads his arms wide and empty. He shakes his head.

"I looked for the gun. I couldn't find it," he says.

"I hid it so the kids wouldn't get it. Here it is." I hold it up so he can see it.

"Oh, Mary," Daddy moans. "It's too late now, Mary."

"Too late for what?"

"Everything. It's all screwed up. I didn't want her to suffer. She's suffered so much. I wanted all of us to be together. You understand that, don't you? You don't hate me, do you, Mary?"

"No, Daddy, I don't hate you." I inch closer to the girls, figuring the distance to Andy, to the door.

"The world's a terrible place, a terrible place," Daddy's saying. "It just smashes you like a bubble. You understand, don't you, Mary? You've always been so grown up. Your mother can't take it. She's too gentle, too fragile."

"Daddy, the girls are going outside now."

"No." He shakes his head wildly, waves the gun. "I promised your mother we'd stay together. I was looking for you, Mary. I couldn't find you. You should've stayed here. I couldn't find you."

"They're going outside now. Do you hear me, Danielle?" I stand between my father and the girls. They're frozen. "Do you hear me, Danielle? Take the girls outside."

"No!" Daddy thunders. "You girls stay here! I'm your father. You do what I tell you! No one listens to me. I tried to tell them: This is a special situation! We're not some scum you can kick out the door! We just need some help! That's all I'm asking—"

"Do you hear me, Danielle? Get out of here! Now!"

She looks at my father and back at me. Then she takes the girls' hands and leads them out.

"Andrew!" Dave calls after the door shuts behind them. "Let me come in there. Let me talk to you, buddy."

"Stay out of here!" my father shouts. "I'm warning you!" He aims the gun at the door and fires.

"Jesus, man, you're blowing it!" Dave shouts.

Daddy covers his face with his hands, the gun trembling near his temples. "Oh, Mary," he groans, "things are so messed up. They won't ever be good again."

"Yes they will. Things are going to be fine. The ambulance will be here any second to take Mama to the hospital." Bright red blood pools beneath her nightgown. She hasn't moved since I came in.

My father looks down at my mother, confused. Horror spreads across his face.

"Oh, Wendy! My God! My God, please help me!" He kneels beside her, whimpering, stroking her hair. "Wendy, darling, can you ever forgive me?" Andy lies beside her, howling. Daddy's face almost breaks with pity.

"You poor little thing. You didn't ask for this, did you. You poor little boy. This is some kind of world. It's not a nice place for a baby, is it."

He reaches for Andy.

"Leave him alone, Daddy."

"I won't leave him alone!" Daddy's on his feet, holding off a mob only he can see. "Leave him alone to be scared and hurt, to be treated like dirt? I promised your mother! I promised her we'd all be together. Now you've spoiled it. You always spoil things, Mary. Why do you always do that?"

"Daddy, I'm coming over there. I'm going to take Andy. You're scaring him."

"No! You can't have him. He's not your son! They take everything you've got and leave you nothing! You're not taking my flesh and blood!"

"I'm taking him, Daddy, and I know you won't hurt me. I'm your daughter and I know you love me."

For a moment my father sees me clearly, his eyes agonized, his face twisted.

"Oh, Mary, oh, honey, it's a crazy old world. It's crazy, you know, the things that can happen. Why is this happening? I don't understand. Mary, I don't understand what's happened."

"Lot's of things happened. But it's going to be fine. They'll take Mama to the hospital and get her all fixed up. Then we'll move to San Francisco and you'll get a job—"

"I'm so sorry, honey. You believe me, don't you? I never meant for any of this to happen." He waves the gun at the RV, at the beach, at Mama. "All I was trying to do was take care of my family. To make them happy. That's all I ever wanted. But no matter what I did, it got all screwed up. And now it's too late. It's too late, Mary."

"No, it's not, Daddy. Please don't make it any worse."

He almost smiles. "Honey, it can't get any worse. And it can't get any better. Forgive me."

He raises his gun. I pull the trigger. My father leaps into the air through the sparkling sprinkler. He is calling my name. He is falling forever. Then the fan of silver water closes around him.

Nineteen

There was so much confusion right after that time. I don't remember a lot of what happened. They say I was in shock.

Aunt Belle keeps telling me it's not my fault.

A helicopter landed on the beach and flew Mama to the hospital. She's still in intensive care. The doctors haven't told her about my father yet. She asks for him but then she forgets; she's on a lot of pain medication.

When the cops came, they were going to arrest me until Dave got in their faces. They almost took him, too. He was screaming.

"For God's sake, the guy went nuts! It was self-defense!" Dave said.

The police asked me, "Who was your father going to shoot? You, himself, the baby?"

I didn't know what he was going to do. I couldn't let him make one more mistake.

They took the kids and me to Child Protective Services and then to a big place out in the country where lots of other kids were staying. Aunt Belle arrived the next day and got us out. The cops said we couldn't go home until the investigation was over, so we checked into a motel.

The newspaper ran big articles about us. Aunt Belle didn't want me to read them, but I did. Daddy was described as a "top executive;" a "broken man driven to despair and desperation by the collapse of his multimillion-dollar insurance empire." He would've liked how important he sounded.

The articles said the Wolfs' Den and the beach were "squalid." They said my sisters' clothes were ragged. Phone calls poured into the county, people wanting to adopt us. Reporters waited outside our motel room, shouting questions whenever we opened the door. TV talk shows invited me to be a guest. Movie producers wanted to buy the rights to my life story.

"What's the matter with you people? Are you out of your minds?" Aunt Belle shouted into the phone, and hung up.

My grandparents flew out and took the girls and Andy home. I had to stay for the investigation. Aunt Belle rented a car and drove me to the county offices for my appointments.

The detectives asked, "Had your father been drinking that morning?"

"I don't know. I don't think so. He never drank in the morning."

"When did he usually drink? In the afternoon? Had he been drinking that night? Was he intoxicated?"

"It's not the way you're making it sound. He's not an alcoholic. He just drinks when he's sad or feeling down in the dumps, or maybe he'll have a beer or two if we're having a barbecue or something."

"Why'd you hide the gun? Did you fear for your life?"

"No, so the girls wouldn't find it."

"He was in the habit of leaving a loaded gun lying around?"

"He never had a gun before we got to that place. Before we got to the beach."

"Why'd he get the gun?"

"I don't know. Sometimes there were strange people around."

"And he taught you how to use it?"

"Yes. So I could take care of the family in case he wasn't there."

"Why wouldn't he be there? Was he planning to be gone?"

"I mean, if he was at work or something. He was going to get a job when we got to San Francisco."

"Were you planning to kill him, when you went into the trailer?"

"Oh, for God's sake," Aunt Belle snapped. "Has everyone gone crazy?"

"Please, ma'am, let her answer the question."

"What kind of question is that? Of course she wasn't planning to kill him. She loved him. He was her father!"

"Please, ma'am, let her answer the question or we'll have to ask you to step outside. Were you planning to shoot him when you went into the trailer, Mary?"

"It's not a trailer; it's an RV. They keep saying it's a trailer in the newspaper."

"Were you planning to shoot him when you went inside?"

"No. I didn't know what he'd done. I didn't know what he'd done until I went inside."

"Why'd you take the gun in there with you?"

"I was afraid. Dave said he'd heard a shot."

Hour after hour I answered their questions. All that time, a tiny voice in my mind whispered: None of this is real. It's not happening.

They made me talk to a psychiatrist, a gray-haired woman. She asked if I hated Daddy.

"No. I love him."

"But you must be very angry at him now."

"Let's say I'm not too happy."

"Did he ever hurt you? Did he ever hit you?"

"Just a couple of times. He didn't mean to."

"Why did he hit you?"

"He was so upset. Everything was falling apart."

"Why were things falling apart?"

"We didn't have any money. We had no place to go. We didn't know what to do."

"You say 'we,' Mary. Did you feel that this was your responsibility, figuring out what your family should do?"

"Well, kind of. I'm the oldest. I try to take care of things."

"What about your mother? Does she take care of things, too?"

"Sometimes. When she can. It's kind of hard to explain."

I could tell that the woman didn't like my parents. She didn't understand that they did the best they could. Okay, so maybe it wasn't so good. They weren't trying to hurt us; they loved us. For a while the cops wanted to charge Mama with neglect because we'd missed a lot of school and there wasn't much food in the RV. Millions of kids go hungry every day. If it's a crime, why doesn't somebody help them?

The psychiatrist said, "Mary, you're just a child. You should never have had so much responsibility. Your parents put you in an impossible situation. Your father even forced you to kill him."

My mind reeled away from the words she was saying. Daddy's dead. He's never coming back. And I will always be the one who killed him.

"Mary, don't you see that he gave you no choice? He'd already shot your mother."

"I didn't want to kill him."

"I know that, Mary."

"I could've shot him in the arm or leg."

But I'm no expert shot, no TV policewoman who could've blown the gun out of his hand. He would've grabbed his wrist and cursed, then come to his senses. Mary, what would I do without you? he would've said.

"This pattern had been developing for years. You were the caretaker and your parents were the children. What they did was wrong. They acted very irresponsibly. Your father's to blame for what happened to him, not you."

He didn't mean to change. It's like tires wearing out. The friction from the road scrapes the rubber thin. Then the tire hits a nail or rock and explodes. It's not the tire's fault.

Forgive me, Daddy.

The psychiatrist wanted to put me on tranquilizers, but I refused. It's hard enough to keep my mind from drifting, back to happy times, even at River's End, my father kissing Mama, tickling Andy's feet; back along those miles of nameless roads, until we're safely home in Nebraska. Daddy gave me my first bike on my sixth birthday, a shiny two-wheeler. It was silver and blue. He jumped through the sprinkler with his hat and clothes on, as if his suit and briefcase weren't important; as if making me laugh was all that mattered.

There was another article in the newspaper today; an interview with the county worker who took Daddy's application.

"He wouldn't answer the questions. He became irrational," said Bob Briggs, intake supervisor. "When I tried to explain that we needed more information, he wouldn't listen. He became very angry. If he'd had a gun then, he would have killed me."

Letters to the editor, calling for tighter gun controls.

Letters arguing that guns don't kill people; people do.

An editorial questioning the welfare system, under the headline: *Could this tragedy have been prevented?*

I will ask myself that question every day of my life.

Grandma called a while ago. She said there were several messages for me on Aunt Belle's phone machine, from someone named Roger Wilson. She said he says he's sorry and he hopes I'm okay; that he'll be in touch again; he's working in Chico.

It took me a moment to realize this was Rocky. He'd never told me his last name.

Grandma said Danielle wanted to talk, and put her on.

I was afraid to hear what she had to say, afraid she'd hate me for killing her father.

"How's it going?" Danielle said.

"Okay. How are you guys doing?"

"All right, I guess. The little kids don't get what's happened. Grandma's told them, but I don't think they understand. I mean, you know, about Daddy."

They have all their lives to try to understand. Maybe someday I will, too.

"How's Andy doing?"

"Fine. Grandma's giving him that mooshy baby food in those little jars. You should smell that stuff. It's disgusting."

"How's it seem to be back there?"

"Okay. Pretty weird. They painted our house. It's a pukey blue. How's Mama doing?"

"All right, I guess. We saw her the other day. She was pretty doped up. They're going to let her out in a couple of weeks."

"I know. Grampa's going back to get her." After a pause Danielle said, "I just wanted to tell you I'm not mad at you. You know, about what happened."

"That's good, Danielle."

"I mean, you couldn't help it. He tried to kill Mama."

I closed my eyes but the picture's in my

mind, engraved in my brain forever; the terrible look of surprise on his face. Then he's falling, falling through time and space, to a place beyond everything but memory.

"I didn't know what to do," I said. "I was afraid he might hurt Andy."

"I know. He just, I don't know, he changed. Why'd he change like that, Mary?"

"Lots of reasons. It's complicated. We'll talk about it when I get home."

"Well, anyway, that's all I wanted to say. I'll see you soon. Here's Grampa."

Before we flew home, I asked Aunt Belle to take me back to River's End.

"I don't think that's such a good idea," she said. She was afraid I couldn't handle it.

"Nothing could be worse than what's happened," I said. I needed to see it one last time.

The beach was closed to campers. All the people were gone. It hadn't been cleaned up yet. There was trash everywhere; shoes, toys, broken bottles, cans, disposable diapers, cars without tires, tires without cars, and the Wolfs' Den, stranded like a shipwreck.

Its blistered sides were tattooed with graffiti. Every window had been smashed; the wind whistled through them. Glass glittered on the sand all around it.

The door was unlocked. It was gutted inside.

Dave helped Aunt Belle store everything we wanted to save. The rest had been stripped; empty drawers and cupboards gaped. There was a hole in the dashboard where the tape deck was missing. Even the coat hangers had been taken.

I was looking for something that was long gone.

Aunt Belle came to the door. She said, "Mary, let's go."

It feels odd to be back in Nebraska. It doesn't feel like home; it's like someplace new. I've seen a few people we used to know. Everybody knows what I did. Some people pity me, some people fear me, I can see it in their eyes. Nobody really knows me.

Aunt Belle says I have to go on with my life and leave the past behind. She says that's what Daddy would have wanted. She wants me to see a counselor, and I will. But the only real answers are in my heart. That's where I talk with my father.

Daddy, wherever you are, I hope you can see us. I hope you know we're going to be all right. I wish so much that things had turned out different. I'll wish that for the rest of my life.

Sometimes I'm so mad at you, I don't know what to do. If I could see you, I'd scream in your face: What's the matter with you? Why couldn't you change? Why couldn't you stop running away? You would've found a job and we'd all be together.

Maybe someday I'll be able to forgive you.

I know you don't blame me, that you'd want me to be happy; to have a good education, a career I enjoy, a home and a family of my own. That's down the road. That's what I want, too.

I'm going to work hard to have a good life, Daddy.

Next week I'm starting school just like you promised.